The Parrot,
Kate and Me

CW00822369

By

Abdul-Majeed Salmasi

Shield Crest

© Copyright 2016 Abdul-Majeed Salmasi

ISBN: 978-1-911090-07-6

A CIP catalogue record for this book
is available from the British Library

MMXVI

Published by
ShieldCrest Publishing Limited
Aylesbury, Buckinghamshire, HP22 5RR
England
www.shieldcrest.co.uk

We often do not appreciate
how valuable animals are to
our life.

AMS

~Dedication~

In memory of my daughter, Zaynab.

~Acknowledgements~

To Dr Ghassan Al-Shaikh Radhi for designing the book cover.

~Preface~

During a trip to Dubai, I was amazed when I saw my nephew kept a pet parrot in his sitting room. I had never had any experience with a parrot before, but when I stayed with my nephew for a few days, I grew an interest in studying that bird and acquired some knowledge of how it was living, behaving and eating. Most importantly was the parrot's ability to mimic humans in the words one may say; it did not take the parrot long to say the words that were repeated. This extended beyond single words to two-three word phrases. It seemed to demonstrate an understanding of behaviour and giving the correct response, such as saying 'bye' each time someone left the premises. I enjoyed seeing the parrot mimicking some acts, such as sneezing or coughing. I was amused at its ability to dance or shake its head, copying my nephew. It seemed as though it enjoyed being played with in such a way.

My nephew's parrot inspired me with the idea of this novel. I began to think whether human use can be made of the parrot's remarkable ability to copy words and actions. I wondered at the further discoveries humans can make of animals' value to mankind. How much have we understood the ability of the parrot and made use of it? Could humans use its remarkable capabilities to benefit society, without causing it harm? It was then that I thought one may obtain some benefits if the parrot is properly trained.

Most importantly this novel points out the purpose of all human beings, even if they seemingly have a disability. If there is a disability in some part of the body, the other senses and body parts are strengthened if put to use. This story explores overcoming the challenges of the psychological dilemmas and depression associated with a disability.

Finally, this novel is fictitious. If there was a similarity in events or names to others, it is a mere co-incidence.

Abdul-Majeed Salmasi
London, UK

~Chapter 1~

Edward

It was a cold Saturday morning in November with the sun spreading its shiny rays over the dry leaves on the trees. Its light reflected the dew drops over the leaves like broken pieces of glass. The rustling sound of the letters dropping through the letter box falling on the floor woke Edward. He sat up yawning then went to draw back the curtains from the window. He wiped a little mist off the cold glass. He then walked to the front door of his apartment and lifted the letters off the floor. He was juggling the envelopes to see where they were from. The first envelope had the sign of the Gas Company in the corner when he commented: 'Oh.. It is a bill.'

Then he looked at the next envelope which seemed to be a junk letter but the third letter grabbed his attention. It was from the Cabinet Office. He was astonished but mumbled sarcastically:

The Prime Minister must be appointing me in his cabinet possibly a Minister.

While trying to open the envelope, he heard the landline telephone ringing. He went to pick it up and heard the voice of a man shouting, "Hello!"

"Yes sir,"

"So it's you?"

"Who is speaking?" said Edward in his regular indifferent manner

"What do you mean by 'who is speaking?' You pretend you don't know me. Don't you?"

"I don't know who you are."

"You are a liar and a crook!"

"Why do you call me a liar and a crook?"

"Because you are one!"

"Well I don't know you and I don't know why you are calling. Why do you call me these names?"

"See how you try to run away from me. It's strange that you pretend you don't know me. Don't you feel ashamed of yourself?"

"Ashamed of myself! Why?"

"Are you trying to be funny? Stop trying to hide the facts

"What facts, sir? I still don't understand what you mean. Please identify yourself."

"That is charming. I identify myself?! Is this how you behave with others too? Listen you... if you"

"I am going to put the receiver down. This is impolite."

"Impolite? If you are not going to pay me the three hundred and fifty pounds which you promised to pay me I shall do ... you won't like me if I continue."

"What three hundred and fifty pounds are you talking about?"

"Again pretend you know nothing about it. This is your nature."

"OK sir I might have forgotten about it. Please explain."

"The faulty car which you sold me two weeks ago. You promised to pay me back three hundred and fifty pounds as a compensation for the fault."

"I am not paying you any money."

"If you are not going to pay me any money I shall call the police or I better come and smash your head."

"If you smash my head you will spend the rest of your life in jail and you won't get any money."

"OK when will you pay me the money? I shall wait till the end of today for settlement."

"I said I shall never pay you any money."

"Why? I am giving you a chance."

"Don't you know why? Because I don't know you and I have never sold you a car."

"Aren't you George Mathew?"

"No I am not."

"Why didn't you say it from the beginning?"

"You didn't give me a chance to explain."

"Sorry."

Then the caller hung up the phone. Although the man on the phone was time-consuming and rude, Ed remained calm. 'Unfortunately this man wasted my time. I feel sorry for him. All he achieved was to raise his blood pressure for no reason.'

That was Ed's personality. He did not show anger over any matter in any circumstance. This was one of the reasons for his success in his work which made him loved by all the employees and bosses. He was quiet and reserved. He was a perfectionist and did not waste time in gossiping or being engaged in useless social matters, or at least that was what he thought they were.

Ed walked back to the letters and picked up the one from the Cabinet office opening the envelope. He read the letter, stared at it then read it again. He raised his head and looked at the letter for a third time and said to himself: 'That can't be true.'

He then stared at the letter again, 'I don't believe it'

Ed smiled sarcastically. 'Why me? That can't be true. How was I chosen amongst thousands of people? This could be a joke. People may try to trick others. I might be chosen by some to be laughed at.'

Ed then put the letter aside and went to the bathroom. After a while he came out and picked up the letter and read it again.

It is Saturday today and the Cabinet Office must be closed. I shall have to phone it on Monday and find out if this is true.

He continued his daily routine. He went to make himself breakfast. He toasted two pieces of bread, boiled two eggs and made coffee. He put them on the dining table and sat down switching on his laptop. He started drinking coffee while searching through his e-mails. Ed then looked at sites for house sale in his area and was talking to himself

"Oh, God. Houses are so expensive! It's difficult to buy a house or even a flat nowadays". He continued eating breakfast and drinking coffee. "It will be impossible for me to get a mortgage with such an expensive housing market with my current savings of only ten thousand pounds"

Ed then switched off the laptop while continuing eating his breakfast.

"I am OK now paying one thousand pounds a month for my rent. I can't save more than two hundred pounds a month," said Ed, standing up taking the empty plate and the mug to the kitchen. "This doesn't bother me. I am happy and satisfied now. I enjoy myself. I love travelling and love history". He washed the plate and the mug and placed them on the rack. He then cleaned the kitchen worktop "Good that I am organised now. Thanks to my late mother and the psychologist whom she took me to in order to make me organised contrary to what I was before"

The sun was filling the kitchen with its strong shiny light. As Ed was about to leave the kitchen he turned his face to check that everything was in place and that all the cupboard doors were closed. He then checked the rubbish bin which was more than half empty. Ed went to the bedroom and put the bed in order then opened the window curtain to allow for the sun to fill the room with its rays. He then opened the window slightly to allow for ventilation.

"I haven't been lucky enough to get married. I am now forty two yet without a partner. I don't think I am bothered. I am married to my work. You can't be married to two wives to a woman and to your work," said Ed, putting on his trousers and his jacket. He then went to the front door and put his trainers on. Ed left the flat after closing the door.

Ed walked briskly in the street as a form of exercise, acquiring enough sunshine in order to build up his vitamin D level as he thought. He stood by the estate agent's windows looking at the properties. He walked to a nearby market where he bought some fruits and fresh vegetables. Ed was concerned about his healthy style of eating and drinking. He never smoked or drank alcohol and ate fresh fruit and vegetables. He avoided eating at restaurants unless he was invited which did not occur often.

On the rest of the Saturday and on Sunday, Ed spent the day at home working on his computer drawing plans for some new projects. On Sunday besides doing his routine 60-minute brisk walking in the street and in the park he had a visit from his only friend and work-mate Ahmad who came to visit him with his wife, Claire, and their eight-year old daughter Farida. They came for afternoon tea. Ed enjoyed their company as he always did. He had known Ahmad for 15 years. Ahmad joined the company where Ed worked during the previous 6 years. Ahmad and Claire often invited Ed to join them for a Sunday lunch. The relation between Ahmad and Ed was very good. At work, Ed was the Head of the Planning Department where Ahmad worked.

~Chapter 2~

United Architects

O n the rainy Monday, Ed left home at 7.00 am on his way to work. This was his habit in order to be at work at 7.45. He avoided traffic as he drove against the flow at that time of the day. Ed was an early starter at work, a habit which he had acquired since childhood; thanks to his late mother who trained him. The big company "United Architects PLC" where Ed had worked for 15 years was situated in Slough. In his office he supervised 12 architects who made plans for rather large projects for various authorities both private and governmental. Their major clients included the Ministry of Defence and the National Health Service. Because of his talents and successes in the first few years when Ed joined the company he was made the Head of his Department in seven years into the job. Since then the company acquired many medals and won numerous bids to make plans for large projects both inland and overseas. This was his fifth year in this position. Ed often made trips to various countries in the Far East, Middle East and Africa. In particular, he made trips to Dubai which was a good market to develop their plans rather successfully. Ed usually continued to work till after 6pm. He enjoyed his work and didn't waste any time in personal matters. At lunch break, he bought a sandwich and ate it while working. He preferred to drink water rather than juice. He organised a meeting once every month when he and his team discussed the most recent advances in the field of architectural engineering. Ed had his own office which was supplied with all the material that was required to make drawings of a project.

Upon arrival and while at his desk on the Monday, Ed was summoned to see the Chairman of the company.

"Ed. I have some good news for you" said the Chairman, Mr Basing.

Ed just nodded his head because the comment did not take him by surprise. He had never received any negative comment from any of his superiors previously.

"Ed. We won the bid to prepare the plan for the highest building in South Africa, the Vasco Da Gama Tower in Cape Town" said Mr Basing with a large smile on his face

"I was expecting that" said Ed with a face full of confidence.

"How many floors were there in your drawing?"

"Two hundred and one"

"Why did you make it 201 and not 200 for instance?" asked Mr Basing in astonishment

"I like my drawings to be odd. It's my style. I believe you know me on this issue" said Ed with a smile of confidence

"Yes I know you but I can't understand why. Probably this is one of the traits which made you successful in your life"

"Thanks. Can I go now?" said Ed while he was trying to leave

"You may sit down please. I want to talk to you" said Mr Basing.

Ed sat down looking at the wall clock placed over the entrance door.

"Are you OK for time?" asked Mr Basing when he saw Ed looking at the clock.

"Not really, Mr Basing" said Ed, looking at Mr Basing

"Shall we have coffee together?" said Mr Basing with a little smile on his face

"I don't fancy drinking much coffee. I had one yesterday", said Ed staring at Mr Basing

"What about tea?" asked Mr Basing, his head was halfway down and raising his eyes to Ed

"Had one this morning. Thanks" said Ed with an indifferent outlook on his face

"Ed. The company's Board of Directors decided to promote you.." said Mr Basing anticipating a reactionary smile from Ed who was staring at Mr Basing

"Yeah" said Ed anticipating that Mr Basing would continue

"It has been decided that you be ....my deputy," said Mr Basing while anticipating a big reaction from Ed

"Apologies Mr Basing. I prefer to stay in my current post as Head of Planning" said Ed without showing any sign of happiness on his face

"Why is that? I have never known of a person rejecting a promotion," said Mr Basing with a look of surprise on his face

"I shall be more productive where I am now. I believe you are in agreement that planning makes the reputation of this company," said Ed who turned his face to check the time on the wall clock

"This promotion is associated with a substantial increase in your salary which I am certain you will welcome. Additionally, you will have shares in the company and you will be called the Deputy Chairman," said Mr Basing

"I would welcome the substantial increase in my salary and having shares in the company but it will be in your company's interest if I remain where I am now. I love my current post," said Ed while standing up and turning to leave the room "I must go now. My team are waiting for me to discuss the new plan for Abu Dhabi's tower"

"But we shall have to discuss this issue again" Said Mr Basing

"Which issue?" said Ed, turning his face to Mr Basing as he was approaching the door to leave the room

"The promotion" said Mr Basing

"I would welcome the increase in the salary. I need it in order to purchase a house" said Ed looking at Mr Basing and standing at the door

"Ed.. It is impossible to have your salary substantially increased without promoting your position in the company...I am afraid," said Mr Basing.

Ed left the office without even thinking about the discussion which he had with Mr Basing. Ed's mind was occupied by the new plan his team was preparing for the new tower in Abu Dhabi. He went to the meeting room where three men and one woman, members of his team, were waiting for him.

"Apologies chaps for being a few minutes late. I was summoned by Mr Basing" Ed said, sitting down at the table. He then started reading the comments received from Abu Dhabi while his team were watching him. There was complete silence while he was reading the comments a few times over.

"God. It's taking him a long time to read just a few lines," whispered the lady member of the team, Amanda, to Ahmad, Ed's friend, who was one of the team members. Ed raised his eyes staring at Amanda. Amanda looked at Ed then lowered her eyes while Ahmad knocked her left foot with his right one.

"Dyslexic people are clever... Amanda" said Ed in a quiet voice then lowered his eyes to continue reading.

"Sorry," said Amanda with a look of embarrassment on her face. After a few minutes of reading the comments by Ed he turned his face to Ahmad

"Ahmad. It seems that our friends in Abu Dhabi do not understand what we have suggested. I think the best solution is for you to pick up the phone and speak to them in Arabic using your Arab way of approach. They might understand you better than our constant written communications. Go and talk to them now" Ed then looked at the wall clock and continued "It's now half past twelve in Abu Dhabi, isn't it?"

Ahmad looked at his wristwatch and said, "Yes, Ed, four hours' difference"

"So they are still at work. Hurry up now," said Ed. Then Ahmad stood up to leave the room

"Ahmad. Be gentle with them. Explain every point that we raised before in detail and get them to agree. Explain why. Call me if you need me. Ahmad, remember we need to win this bid. We must win this bid"

Ed continued discussing other issues with his team while Ahmad was on the phone in his office talking to the authorities in Abu Dhabi. After 15 minutes Ahmad entered the room with a smile on his face

"They agreed to our suggestions. This is good news," said Ahmad, sitting down

"Just like I said," said Ed to the rest of the team. "We shall win this bid. I can tell you"

At the end of a long working day for Ed, he left the office at 8.10 pm driving his car back to his apartment in Acton. It was just before 9 pm when he entered his apartment. He put his brief case with his laptop on the table then went to the deep freezer to get a frozen fish out which he placed in the oven after putting some oil on. After a quick shower he went to check the fish in the oven but it was still not cooked enough so he was about to sit down when he saw the letter from the Cabinet Office which he received on Saturday.

"Oh, dear. I forgot to phone the Cabinet Office," said Ed without expressing much interest. Then he put the letter aside and went to take out the fish after switching off the oven.

~Chapter 3~

Buckingham Palace

Ten days had passed since Ed received the letter from the Cabinet Office. He still had not phoned the Office to check the truth of its contents. On Monday he took the letter with him to his workplace planning to phone the Cabinet Office. As soon as he arrived and sat down in his office at five minutes after eight, he heard a knock on his door

"Come in" said Ed, switching on his computer. The door was opened. Ed had his back towards the office door facing his computer screen.

"Good morning, Ed". It was the voice of Mr Basing, the Chairman of the company

"Good Morning Mr Basing.."said Ed with a look of surprise on his face. This was the first time Mr Basing had come to Ed's office

"I think it would be much better if you came to my office," said Mr Basing. This was the first time Mr Basing had come personally to ask Ed into his office. Ed stood up and went to accompany Mr Basing.

"After you," said Mr Basing which took Ed by surprise.

"Mr Basing. It seems your secretary is not in yet," said Ed, walking down the corridor

"She is here," said Mr Basing. This was even more surprising to Ed, because Mr Basing had come personally to summon him to his office. Mr Basing entered the office after allowing Ed to enter then asked Ed to sit down on the sofa. Mr Basing sat beside him.

"Yes, Mr Basing," said Ed

"Ed... have you had any thoughts?" asked Mr Basing

"Thoughts? About what?" said Ed with a look of surprise on his face

"You seem to be very busy," said Mr Basing "I'm talking about your promotion, to be my deputy, as decided by the Board of Directors"

"I told you Mr Basing, I can't accept it because I don't want to leave my responsibility as Head of the Planning Team. My current position serves your company much better than if I were to become your deputy," said Ed

"But you would have a substantial increase in your salary and own shares in the company. I don't think anyone would reject this offer...except you"

"Mr Basing, I would welcome the increase in my salary which would help me to buy a house, but my career is all based upon what I achieve in my unit with my team," said Ed very calmly

"Ed. We shall have a compromise. You shall become my deputy while continuing being Head of your Team. How about that?" said Mr Basing with a smile on his face looking at Ed as he was waiting for a positive answer from Ed

"That I can accept or rather consider"

"Why consider and not accept?" asked Mr Basing, smiling more broadly

"I shall have to ask Ahmad who is an eminent member of my team to be my deputy as I am certain I shall have numerous responsibilities if I become the Deputy Chairman. I am sure he will accept and especially if we increase his salary. He deserves it because he is efficient and knowledgeable"

"That can be arranged and is not a problem if that is your condition for acepting the new post," said Mr Basing with a big smile on his face

"When will this new position be effective from?" asked Ed

"From now! I shall ask my PA to type the offer letter to you now and the new contract will be issued by HR today for you to sign," said

Mr Basing "You will have to move offices to the one next to mine"

"Thanks, Mr Basing," said Ed, standing up to leave the office

"Please call me John"

"OK"

"Sit down, Ed, we haven't finished yet," said Mr Basing. Ed sat down. "Do you know the result of our bid for Abu Dhabi's tower?"

"No" said Ed

"How did it go?"

"I'm not sure, but we tried hard. We tried our best. Ahmad did a lot of work on it especially in communicating directly with Abu Dhabi"

"Well, we won the bid. I have just received an e-mail" said John Basing

"Congratulations, John. I must inform my team. We shall have to celebrate"

"Yes, I agree. There is another matter, which is the most important. This one we have to celebrate," said John Basing

"What's that?" asked Ed, raising his head to stare at Mr Basing with surprise

"That is strange! Didn't you don't know about it" said Mr Basing

"I know about it? About what?" said Ed with surprise

"Because it concerns you!" said John

"Concerns me? I don't understand," said Ed, staring at Mr Basing

"You should be the first one to know about it," said Mr Basing

"Know about it? From where?" said Ed calmly and quietly

"It is in the papers and was announced on television," said Mr Basing

"I can't understand what you mean," said Ed looking at Mr Basing

"You really surprise me" said Mr Basing placing his left middle finger and the left index over his lips "I don't understand how you could be so oblivious."

"John. I still don't understand" said Ed

"Our company is now pleased to announce that the Deputy Chairman and Deputy Managing Director of United Architect PLC is..." said John as he was waiting for his sentence to be continued by Ed

"Edward James Carpenter" said Ed after waiting a few seconds for John to continue

"No, it's not Edward James Carpenter," said Mr Basing staring at Ed with a knowing smile.

"I thought you had just appointed me" said Ed

"Yes but you are not Edward James Carpenter," said Mr Basing with a smile

"Who am I then?" asked Ed

There was a short period of silence as the two men stared at each other. Then Mr Basing said, "You will be .... Sir Edward James Carpenter"

"So the letter I received from the Cabinet Office was right in what it said?" said Ed

"When did you receive this letter?" asked John

"About 10 days ago, but I thought it was a trick. I was meant to phone the Cabinet Office but I forgot. I brought the letter with me today to contact them," said Ed

"No need to phone. It is in the papers today," said John "You will soon be bombarded by the press, television and radio. It's therefore important that you will be my deputy as from today...Sir Edward"

"Well I am not Sir yet until I am officially knighted," said Ed

"You will soon receive a letter from Buckingham Palace inviting you to attend the ceremony. After that we shall have to change our headed letters and our website to include your name as Sir Edward" said Mr Basing happily

Ed then went to his office and it was Amanda who came first to congratulate him. Soon the news spread in the company and Ed spent the day receiving congratulations from his colleagues. The letter appointing him as Deputy Chairman and a contract were issued in the afternoon. He signed the documents happily and moved to his new office. Ahmad was appointed Deputy Head of the Planning Team.

It was a great and tiring day for Ed in the office. At the end of the day he found himself heading towards a great deal of responsibilities especially now that John Basing was planning to go away on a business trip to Singapore and Japan for a week. Ed went home at the end of the day with a stack of paper work. He picked up the letter from the Cabinet Office and looked at it then smiled.

"It's nice to be knighted by the Queen," said Edward after a deep sigh

"I never thought that one day I would be receiving such an honour. Sir Edward. And if I were married, my wife would have been Lady Carpenter". Ed shook his head with a little smile on his face opening his eyes wide staring at the letter he had received from the Cabinet Office. He then bent forward to take the letter between the fingers of his left hand. "I wonder how I should be kneeling down when the Queen lays the sword on my shoulders. I wonder whether being left-handed is going to make a difference." While he was walking to the kitchen to make himself a cup of tea, he changed direction and went towards the sitting room. When his eyes fell on the picture of his mother, he stood staring at it. Then he walked along to the picture and stopped only 2 feet away from it, with a mild smile on his face followed by a slight nod, pursing his lips.

"Mum. You never believed I will one day become a Sir Edward" said Ed to his mother's picture hanging on the wall. "My teachers always thought I was a failure because I was dyslexic. You were very sad for your only child being treated like that. I remember you often cried for me. Nevertheless, you struggled to encourage me. After working hard during the day, you used to spend a long time in the evenings to revise my lessons with me. I still remember the day I came back from the school carrying a letter from the school to say I was hopeless. I was only eight. You hugged me, put me on your lap, and said to me don't worry, one day you will prove to be the opposite; you are not hopeless. You kept saying you are bright and clever. You will be successful in your life. It was then that I felt different and encouraged. One thing you didn't like about me was that I was disorganised and apprehensive. You managed to alter that completely. You took me to a psychologist who after sessions and sessions managed to make the change. Here I am now. I feel I am organised and not apprehensive. It was your courage and struggle which made all the changes. May God bless your soul" Then he walked away a few steps towards the kitchen but only to turn back to his mother's picture and walk towards it again and face it.

"You looked after me especially after my dad had passed away. You worked very hard in the local Council so that I could continue my education in good schools. I wish you were alive now to see me being knighted by the Queen. You would have accompanied me to Buckingham Palace. I have never entered the Palace previously but I am sure it will be exciting"

Ed sat down and relaxed. He was so excited because of the knighthood. He still couldn't understand the reason why he was in receipt of such an honour from the Queen. His memories went back to his childhood. He remembered the days when his mother hoped that Ed would become a doctor. She encouraged him to study and bought him everything he needed for his education. He was slow in reading during his early days at school until he was diagnosed with dyslexia. His schoolmates often laughed at him and made fun of him especially as he was the only left-handed pupil. They made him believe he was disabled. He grew up as calm and quiet because he always thought himself inferior to the others. The pupils took advantage of his weaknesses and often addressed him as "stupid," "retard" and "dumb". One day when he was in high school a few pupils decided to gather around him and attack him. He was subsequently involved in a fight defending himself. It was decided following a subsequent investigation, where the pupils gave false evidence about him, that Ed should be suspended from school for one week. This particular incident was the reason why he was rejected from entrance to medical schools. He subsequently studied biomedical sciences hoping to enter medical school after graduation. However, because his mother died when he was in the third year of university, he lost interest in continuing to study medicine. The death of his mother was a big shock to him and made a big change in his life. He felt he was lost in life and became depressed for a few months. After his mother's death he realised that he had been deeply attached to her. He thought his life was worthless without her. He felt very lonely. He had become interested in hypnosis and hypnotherapy while studying biomedical sciences and after graduation. Because Ed was artistic, he decided to study architectural engineering. When he graduated as an architectural engineer, he found a job in a company in Yorkshire where he stayed for three years, during which he advanced in his job because of his creative ability. Ed used his background knowledge in neurolinguistic programming to build up good relations with his fellow employees and clients at work.

Ed's main strength was his power of imagination which he used in order to design buildings. When he was 30 years old he joined United Architects PLC as an architect and proved to have talent and capability. After six years he became Head of the Planning Team where he stayed till he was promoted to Deputy Chairman. During his time with United Architects Ed managed to increase the profits of the company significantly. The company became well known all over the Far East and the Middle East where some big projects designed and produced by Ed were marketed. This was in addition to some national projects within the UK which were mainly designed by Ed and his team. For these reasons, Ed's name appeared in the New Year Honour list where he was on the list for Knighthood.

A few days later Ed received a letter from Buckingham Palace inviting him to attend the Palace for the Knighthood ceremony. Although he was happy, he was saddened because his mother was not alive to see him being knighted by the Queen.

Ed attended the knighthood ceremony at Buckingham Palace. In the hall while Her Majesty the Queen was standing on the stage to knight five candidates, Ed was the third candidate. He was knighted for his profound services to the country and British society and the community. Ed was nervous when he was called. He had to kneel on his right knee before the Queen who then knighted him. Subsequently Ed was interviewed by various TV channels and press. In the New Year, he returned to his work as Sir Edward James Carpenter. A new sign carrying his name was placed on the door of his office. The headed letters and the website of the company were changed to include the name of Sir Edward James Carpenter.

The United Architects Company PLC organised a reception party for the new Deputy Chairman Sir Edward Carpenter because of the knighthood. The party was attended by all the employees and members of the Board of Directors in addition to the Mayoress of Berkshire, local MPs and Councillors, some eminent local people and community leaders. Sir Edward gave a speech of welcome in which he said, "...I am proud to be knighted not just for the sake of being addressed as Sir Edward but mainly to prove to people that a less capable person in society with some form of illness like dyslexia should not be thought of as an" invalid" or disabled. People with any form of disability should be encouraged to progress throughout their lives and be productive. If you have inability in one of your many powers or senses, remember you have more than dozens of others to compensate. My late mother, may God bless her soul, always wanted me to be a medical doctor. She worked very hard as a single parent after the death of my father in order to enable me to finish my education. Unfortunately or rather fortunately, I could not, for some reason, enter medical school but instead I studied biomedical sciences hoping to study medicine after graduation. But after my mother had passed away, I changed my mind. After graduation I decided to study what I was good at namely Architectural Engineering. Now here I am an architect with a background of biomedical sciences which I find very useful to design buildings for the National Health Service in the United Kingdom and other Health authorities all over the world. When I was in school, my fellow pupils used to address me as "dumb" and "stupid" because I was slow in reading and understanding. I was laughed at because I was left-handed. What gave me the strength to convert those remarks into a completely opposite perception was my mother's repeated encouraging sentence of "Don't listen to what they say because you are clever". I therefore paid no attention to what was said. I just used to switch off my hearing to the way in which I used to be addressed. This is what I have learnt in my life: do what you think suits you best and don't pay attention to what is said about you"

We all have heard about Albert Einstein, one of the greatest scientists in this world and the founder of the theory of relativity. Who would believe that the dyslexic Einstein was to become what he became? Einstein's teachers said he was "mentally slow, unsociable and drifts in his foolish dreams" and labelled him as mentally handicapped. Einstein did not speak till he was four. Nor did I. Einstein did not read till he was seven. So did I. Einstein said that most teachers wasted their time by asking questions that were intended to discover what a pupil did not know, whereas the true art of questioning was to discover what the pupil did know or was capable of knowing. I also quote from Einstein "Everybody is a genius but if you judge a fish by its ability to climb a tree it will remain all its life believing that it is stupid". I quote from one of the famous dyslexics: "I don't suffer from dyslexia, I live with it. I suffer from the ignorance of people who think they know what I can and cannot do". Here I am today, a dyslexic standing amongst people who are not dyslexic but I still don't know what your thoughts are about me. A teacher sent a note home with a six-year old boy saying he was too stupid to learn. That boy was Thomas Alva Edison, the great inventor, the founder of the electric lamp, cinematograph and the gramophone. I am sure you heard of George Washington, Tom Cruise, Steven Spielberg, Sir Richard Branson, Beethoven, Agatha Christie, Walt Disney, Bill Gates, Benjamin Franklin, Henry Ford, The Boxer Mohammad Ali, and the famous doctor John Horner. Those famous names from different kinds of professions were all dyslexic. My final advice is not to listen to what other people say about you. You can be what you want to be if you are following the right track."

His speech was met by a huge standing ovation.

~Chapter 4~

The Parrot

After the knighthood, Ed had numerous visits by journalists and was interviewed by many television and radio channels. Following the interviews and journalists' visits a significant increase in the requests by various organisations and establishments for project planning was noticed. Although Ed was seriously considering purchasing a house, he was unable to proceed because he was not in possession of a suitable amount for a deposit. Accordingly he decided to wait until he had enough savings. However his only concern was that an increase in the price of the properties might have occurred if he had to wait till he had a sufficient amount of money in his savings. He therefore decided to approach Mr Basing for a loan, which was welcomed by Mr Basing, who decided to offer him an interest free loan of £150,000. Ed was very pleased and started looking for a house in or around Slough at close proximity to his place of work. The lack of free time was the only obstacle to halt him from a speedy and immediate search for accommodation. Accordingly he decided to acquire the loan only in the event of an agreement reached to purchase a property.

Ed's friend Ahmad who became in charge of the Planning Team began to practise his managerial ability and was learning to progress in his new career. Ahmad was pleased with his new task which in turn allowed more time for Ed to function as a Deputy Chairman. Mr Basing who was 64 years old was pleased with Ed taking the new position and this in turn led to the surrender of his numerous responsibilities to Ed. However, Ed continued his interest in planning and was meeting with his team once weekly and offering them his expert advice. The final decision making of the planning team remained in the hands of Ed.

Two weeks after Ed's knighthood, Ahmad came to visit him at home on a Sunday afternoon. When the bell rang at his apartment at 4.00pm on the Sunday, Ed opened the door to find Ahmad alone. Neither his wife, Claire, nor his daughter Farida was accompanying him. Ahmad, who was carrying a large cage containing a bird, entered the apartment

"Where is the rest of the family?" asked Ed, closing the door

"Farida is ill and Claire is staying with her," replied Ahmad, entering the apartment and sitting down

"Sorry to hear about this. I hope it's not serious," said Ed, sitting down

"No, it's the usual children's matters. A viral infection with a temperature," replied Ahmad. "Ed, please accept my warmest congratulations on your knighthood. Well deserved. The Company must be proud that you became the Deputy Chairman. Ed, honestly I was thinking seriously of what gift should I bring you.."

"Come on, Ahmad. We are close friends. It's enough for me to have your support," said Ed, trying to put the coffee table near where Ahmad was sitting.

"You are single. I thought a companion would suit you nicely," said Ahmad with a smile on his face

"Will you get me a wife as a gift?" said Ed with a big smile on his face

"I wish I could, Ed," replied Ahmad "I thought of this nice companion here." Ahmad lifted the cage. "This is a parrot which I bought yesterday for you. It's one of the best and finest species, known as African Grey. It's a great talker"

"Many thanks indeed, Ahmad. This is really great." Ed held the cage and looked at the parrot with a look of happiness and a smile on his face.

"I know you don't fancy a dog," said Ahmad

"Or a cat or any other pet. I am certain I shall have a great time with this great talker," replied Ed. "At least it will keep me company. But it will need looking after."

"It's not draconian, Ed," said Ahmad "It doesn't need a great deal of care. It's cheap to run. You might need to take it to the vet once every 2 months although I have done all the initial vaccinations. Here is the certificate and a little book giving you some information on the biology and how to handle it" Ahmad gave a small book and the certificate to Ed which he took and looked at quickly.

"This will be my bed-time readings" said Ed, putting the book and the certificate on a chair beside him. He looked at the parrot and started making a series of brief whistling sounds to it.

"It won't talk if people are talking around it...usually. However you should say words repetitively on two or three successive days and later it will repeat what you said. Some people say it will even imitate coughing or sneezing" said Ahmad

"I feel sorry for this poor animal sitting in this cage. We are restricting its freedom. It's like someone in prison. You don't like to be imprisoned, do you?" said Ed

"I know you are good-hearted and too nice. But you can let the parrot out of the cage if you so wish to move around in the flat"

"Now let us forget about this bird and make some tea. Do you want to have some sandwiches with me? I bought you some halal chicken and made you a nice chicken sandwich. I was expecting Claire and Farida to come too," said Ed, going the Kitchen.

Ahmad followed Ed and both started making tea. Ed opened the fridge and took the sandwiches out then sat with Ahmad in the kitchen to eat and to drink the tea.

"Incidentally, Ed. Your speech at the reception the other day was great and very informative. It had lots of messages," said Ahmad proudly.

"I am glad you liked it"

"Yes, Ed. You should have heard what people were saying about you and your speech," said Ahmad "Now that you have become the Deputy Chairman of this big company and Sir Edward, aren't you thinking of getting married? Forgive me for asking you this personal question, but I am your friend," said Ahmad, drinking his tea

"My friend? You are the only friend I have," said Ed. "To be honest with you I haven't yet found the suitable partner. I wish

Claire your wife had a sister whom I would have considered. In this way I should have behaved like you Arabs. I like your habits and customs"

"Yes, Ed. You are right. Claire is a wonderful wife and is now behaving like an Arab after mixing with my family. You can see she cooks Arabic dishes all the time and can speak Arabic. Claire is very supportive to me. As it is said, there is a woman behind each great man"

"I haven't been lucky enough to find a suitable partner yet. I am now forty-two and the more advanced in age you are, the more difficult it will be to find a suitable partner. This is especially true when I am busy at work, as I am now," said Ed. "Have some sandwiches. This is the best I could do. I hope you like them"

In the subsequent days, Ed began to read about parrots. He bought some nuts and sunflower seeds and placed them in the cage and started observing how the parrot enjoyed eating them. He practised tapping and massaging the back of the parrot's head with his index and middle fingers which the parrot enjoyed. Ed was eager to hear the parrot saying some words. He came near the cage and repeatedly said "Hello. How are you?" After a while as he was going away to the kitchen he heard a sound of "Hello". He thought it was coming from outside. Then he heard it again but when he came to the sitting room there was no sound. Ed then went to the kitchen again to bring the cup of coffee which he had made. He heard the sound of "Hello" again. Ed was very pleased when he realised it was coming from the parrot.

Ed's mobile phone rang. He picked it up to learn it was Ahmad. He spent 15 minutes on the phone. When he finished the call, Ed went to the kitchen to hear the parrot saying "Ahmad" repeatedly but it stopped when Ed came to the sitting room again. He learnt that the parrot talked only if no one was around it in the room.

The parrot wouldn't go to sleep if there was a noise or it was light. Ed learned to wrap the cage with a cloth to make it dark enough and ensured enough quietness for the parrot to go to sleep. In the morning the parrot woke up either by the noise of Ed moving about or if Ed removed the cloth surrounding the cage. Gradually Ed became used to the parrot which soon became an essential of Ed's daily routine and life. Every time Ed left the flat he heard "Bye" from the parrot but the words it said repeatedly were "Ahmad", "How are you?", "plan", and "structure".

~Chapter 5~

The Project

Following Ed's knighthood and appointment as the Deputy Chairman of the company, a noticeable increase was noted in the number of requests for big projects from all over the world with a new market developing from South America. For the first time in the history of the company it received requests for plans from Venezuela and Brazil. Ed had to make a trip to Brazil while John Basing made a separate trip to Venezuela.

Because of his busy work schedule, Ed was unable to continue looking for a suitable property to purchase and that task began to fade away from his plans at the time. He had returned to his apartment at 10.00pm on a Friday after a tiring day when he heard his mobile phone ringing with an unidentified caller. He picked up the phone to hear a lady's voice

"Hello. Is this Sir Edward James Carpenter?" said the lady on the phone

"Yes, it is, Madam. Who is speaking?" said Ed

"I am Mrs Jackson, the PA to Mr Davies the Energy Secretary" said the lady on the phone

"Will you please stop annoying me at this time of the evening? I have so many things to do and I am not prepared to receive bogus calls or jokes" said Ed and put the telephone down.

Soon the phone rang again with an unidentified number. Ed answered "Hello"

"Sir Edward, please listen. This is not a bogus call. I got the.." said the lady on the phone but soon was interrupted by Ed, who replied

"I told you lady whoever you are; I am not prepared to receive jokes and bogus calls. I am so busy and have enough on my plate," said Ed who then switched off his telephone to avoid such calls and went to the kitchen to make himself a cup of tea. Then he heard the parrot saying "Hello" repeatedly. Ed smiled and came to see the parrot with the cup of tea in his hand.

"See. Now people are trying to make fun and play jokes on me. Do you agree, my dear parrot? I don't think you do," said Ed talking to the parrot "I think your water cup is empty. You need some water don't you?"

As Ed was trying to take the empty water cup from the cage, he heard the landline telephone ringing. Ed left the cup in the cage and went to pick up the phone:

"Hello"

"Is that Sir Edward James Carpenter?" said a man's voice

"Yes. Who is speaking?" said Ed with surprise on his face

"I am William Davies the Energy Secretary.." said the caller

"Listen, I told the lady who called me on my mobile a minute ago, and who claimed to be the PA to the Energy Secretary, that I am so busy and am not prepared to receive jokes or bogus calls. I am so busy and don't want to listen to non-sense. If you have nothing else to do, please stop annoying me. Please do not call me again" said Ed in a quiet mood and put the receiver down "I don't know where these people got my phone numbers from. They are silly and have nothing else to do except annoying people." He then went to take the cup from the parrot's cage

"I think I should change my telephone numbers. Another task to do," said Ed putting the cup full of water in the cage. Because he was working on reviewing some plans, Ed did not go to bed until 3.00 am.

At 10.00 am. on the following day, Saturday, Ed woke up to the sound of the doorbell which was ringing repeatedly.

"OK...OK, give me a moment," shouted Ed as he was leaving the bed and putting his trousers on. The bell rang again. Ed rushed to the door and opened it to see two tall well-dressed men with ties on looking at him.

"Good morning, Sir" said one of the men very politely

"Good morning. Yes. Can I help you?" said Ed with a surprise on his face

"Are you Sir Edward James Carpenter?" asked the other man

"Yes, I am. Who are you?" said Ed

"Can you accompany us please?" said one of the men

"Accompany you?" said Ed with an insincere smile on his face and a look of apprehension." Where to?"

"To meet the Energy Secretary. He is waiting for you," said one of the two men

"Ha..ha..? A joke, ha? And what does his Excellency want from me?" said Ed sarcastically

"We thought he spoke to you last night and that you were expecting us," said one the two men

"Listen, sir or sirs I don't have time to receive jokes and sarcasm," said Ed trying to shut the door in the face of the two men. The door was immediately prevented from being closed by the arm of one of the two men and his foot against it.

"Sir Edward, we shall allow you fifteen minutes to make yourself ready and to accompany us. We shall wait here outside. Fifteen minutes only as the Energy Secretary is waiting for you and there isn't enough time," said one of the two men. Then he shut the door.

Ed realised that he had to get changed and make himself ready. He went to his bedroom.

"Who says these men are truthful in what they claim? Couldn't this be a trap or a trick?" Ed mumbled to himself. He opened the wardrobe and took a suit out but he stopped and picked up the landline telephone trying to make a call.

"I must call the police and see if this is true or a bogus invitation".

Ed's landline telephone was dead. He then went to his mobile telephone to discover it needed recharging. He stood up and didn't know what to do next to save himself from that dilemma. He was apprehensive but then he realised that he had forgotten to ask the two men for identification. He then finished dressing and went to the door and opened it in apprehension to see the two men waiting for him with smiles on their faces.

"Can I ask you for your ID please?" asked Ed in apprehension

The two men showed their ID. Ed realised they were security officers working in the Department of Energy

"I haven't had my breakfast yet or even a cup of tea," said Ed

"You can have it with his Excellency," said one of the two men

Ed then realised he had to accompany them although he was still in doubt of their mission.

The two men accompanied Ed to the ground floor and went to their black car where one of them went to the driver's seat while the other opened the back door to allow Ed to sit in the back seat. After shutting the door, the man went to sit in the front seat beside the driver. Throughout the drive Ed was in doubt and apprehension. He had various thoughts as to what the aim of those two men was. Did they have a bogus mission? Did they want to kidnap him for a ransom? If it was a kidnap, what was the reason? He wasn't a politician or was involved in problems or political mission. Ed knew that there was no relation at all between his job and the Department of Energy. Various questions were circulating in his mind till he arrived at the Department of Energy where the car stopped outside its main entrance. He felt comfortable upon arrival but was still doubtful. One of the men came round and opened the door. Ed accompanied him to the building then to the office of the Energy Secretary's PA. He entered the room to be welcomed by the PA who introduced herself.

"I am Emma Jackson, the PA to the Energy Secretary" said the lady extending her hand to shake Ed's

"So it was you, madam, who spoke to me over the phone last night?" said Ed, shaking hands with Mrs Jackson

"Yes, indeed," said Mrs Jackson with a smile on her face

"So it wasn't a bogus call as I thought. I could not figure out why someone from the Department of Energy was calling me at 10 o'clock in the evening. I cannot understand why I in particular am summoned by the Energy Secretary" said Ed with a very serious face

"Never mind, Sir Edward. I couldn't disagree with you at all," said Mrs Jackson. "If you would kindly take a seat for a minute, please".

Mrs Jackson then entered the office of the Energy Secretary and shut the door behind her. Ed was looking around at the walls and the desk questioning with himself the purpose and the reasons for him being summoned by the Energy Secretary. Soon Mrs Jackson opened the door and asked Ed to enter, holding the door open.

"Sir Edward.. please come in," said Mrs Jackson

Ed entered the office and soon the Energy Secretary left his seat, stood up and came towards Ed to shake hands with him

"I am William Davies. Most welcome, Sir Edward and thanks for sparing us your valuable time. I do apologise for the way you were summoned to us. We spoke last night over the phone," said Mr Davies, who with his right hand was motioning to Ed to sit on the settee beside him.

"I do apologise, Mr Davies. I thought it was a bogus call. I have to be careful; especially in these days" said Ed

"That's OK, Sir Edward. It makes me happy to learn you are so vigilant. You will soon find out why we called you," said Mr Davies

"I am still wondering why you are happy," said Ed with a look of astonishment on his face

"Yes, Sir Edward. It means that you are very careful with whom you speak to and from whom you receive calls and whom you have contacts with. This is important from the safety point of view," said Mr Davies with a large smile on his face.

"I don't understand!" said Ed with surprise

"Soon you will understand, Sir Edward," said Mr Davies "How about tea or coffee? Have you had your breakfast?"

"Not yet. I woke up to the doorbell ringing with your men on the doorstep. It's not my habit to wake up late but because I was working till the early hours of this morning I overslept" said Ed

"We know you are very active and a workaholic, Sir Edward" said Mr Davies

"It seems you have a full knowledge of my life, Mr Davies," said Ed with a mild smile. He now felt more comfortable

"So I understand you didn't have breakfast?" said Mr Davies

"Not yet. I don't fancy a breakfast but probably a cup of coffee will do me fine" said Ed

"No. We shall have breakfast together. I shall ask Mrs Jackson to get it ready. It will only take five minutes to prepare," said Mr Davies, who then stood up to pick up one of the three telephones on his desk and spoke with Mrs Jackson

"Breakfast for Sir Edward and me please," said Mr Davies who then put the receiver on.

"Sir Edward. Our sincere apologies for the way we invited you to come and without much prior notice. This is for security reasons, and you will learn why. We shall discuss things over breakfast. Shall we go now?"

Ed stood up and accompanied Mr Davies to another room through the PA's office where there was a round table with a few chairs round it. There were juice and water, bread, butter, cheese and honey and jam for two people. Mr Davies asked Ed to sit down and he sat too.

"Would you like tea or coffee? Both are available," asked Mr Davies, pointing out two pots on the table. Ed helped himself to tea.

"I too like tea in the morning" said Mr Davies and both started to eat breakfast and drink juice and tea

"Sir Edward. I am very much aware how loyal you are to your work. Your speech on the evening of the reception organised at your company in celebration of your knighthood was very impressive" said Mr Davies with a smile

"You were not present. Were you there when I gave the speech?" Asked Ed with a surprise on his face

"No, I wasn't there, but some friends and journalists told me. You seem to be very loyal to your country, the United Kingdom," said Mr Davies

"A successful person in his work especially when he receives that honour from the Queen, must be loyal to his country. This is not questionable," said Ed, drinking tea

"Sir Edward. We shall now broach the subject which I wanted to discuss with you. We have a big project which will serve the United Kingdom as a country and its people and we would very much love your contribution. I must use another broader word than contribution. Let us say we would love you to be involved in it," said Mr Davies

"I am prepared for any involvement within my own capacity to serve the United Kingdom and the British people. Who are the 'we' you mention?" asked Ed

"I mean the Government, but your involvement will serve the country and not our party or the Government. We are aware that loyal people like you will be pleased to provide the service; it will not make any difference whichever party is ruling. A project to serve the nation is not a party's project but is for the country" said Mr Davies

"It depends upon the project itself. If it were," said Ed, raising his two hands to give the signs of two inverted commas, "election propaganda then it would be a different matter"

"I will not disagree with you at all on that" said Mr Davies "I am not going to discuss the project with you today but will tell you it's a great British project which will be based in the UK but will serve the UK population and the country as I said. Physicists and scientists produced the idea but now we need someone like your good self to make the plans and the structures"

"The best way is to approach my company. Our company is huge, well known and highly reputable. Beside it has all the resources" said Ed

"This is the problem. This is the reason why we wanted to talk; just you and me. Because of the project's importance and it's being top secret the Prime Minister and I decided to approach you at person and ask you if you and only you can do the work privately on your own and at your own spare time in your own residence," said Mr Davies, anticipating a positive answer from Ed.

"Why me personally? There are thousands of architects in this country. Why me? asked Ed with surprise

"What a question! You seem to be rather humble and modest. Your reputation as one of the best architects in this country and in the world is a good reason. You are an asset and a big representative of the United Kingdom in your field in the world. Also important is the fact that you are single and don't have a partner. That helps not to expose the secret of the plan to anyone," said Mr Davies.

"Mr Davies. Do you think if I were married or had a partner she would know about what I was doing, especially if it was secret and of a national security nature?" asked Ed

"Well that statement does help, but your situation as someone without a partner and not in a relationship is very helpful and seems to be a good co-incidence," said Mr Davies

"So if I am getting married tomorrow it will make the project or the plan void. Won't it?" asked Ed

"Not at all, but what I meant is it does help. Now Sir Edward, after this introduction. What do you think? Will you be able to do the plan as we require single-handed and privately? It's a huge project and might take a very long time. I am not going to ask you to give me your verdict now. Shall we leave it till next Saturday? If you are agreeable we shall have a prolonged discussion in this office again at a breakfast next Saturday. How about that?" asked Mr Davies

"Yes I agree. I shall give it some thought and see how I can cope with this," said Ed

"I hope you can come back with a positive answer" said Mr Davies with a smile on his face

"What if I disagree? Not because of any unwillingness but because of time constraints. I have numerous responsibilities in my current job," said Ed, who looked very serious

"If it was because of time constraints then I suggest you leave it to us; we can find a solution," said Mr Davies with confidence

"Solution?!" said Ed with great surprise "How?"

"I think we should leave the answer till we know if you refuse because of this reason. Sir

Edward, you were selected because you are an excellent unique architect who has been very successful in his planning and designs and who we think would be the best man to do this job. If there is any difficulty we will be able to resolve it in order to secure the time to do the work," said Mr Davies quietly

Ed stood up to leave. Mr Davies shook hands with him

"Please, Mr Davies. If I decide to come and meet next week, I don't want the same way of summoning me. I can come on my own. I know the way"

"We prefer that you come in the same way with two of our men. It's better for security reasons but you will be informed beforehand," said Mr Davies, giving Ed his personal card "Here is my card where you can see my private mobile telephone number. Please contact me directly any time when you need me. Equally please allow me to do the same when I need to. I hope you agree"

Ed took the card happily "Thank you" He was leaving the room

"Incidentally, Sir Edward. Just to let you know that the remuneration for this project will be very rewarding and negotiable once you have agreed," said Mr Davies "You will be escorted by the same men back home. They are nice people"

"I will be used to them soon," said Ed with a little smile on his face.

As Ed was leaving he was welcomed by the same two men who accompanied him to the car back to his flat. While he was in the car, he was thinking about the new project which he regarded as a new venture. On the one hand he regarded it as a challenge for his career especially since it was serving the nation and the British people as he was told by the Energy Secretary. On the other hand his only obstacle was the enormous amount of responsibility he had in his company. He thought that the best way to do it besides working on Saturday and Sunday was to take a few weeks' holiday from work, which he deserved.

As soon as Ed arrived home he placed his mobile phone on the charger. Then he picked up the receiver of the landline telephone and tried to dial the telephone number of Ahmad, which he had not memorised. He went to his bedroom and fetched little old telephone book which he had had for a long time. He opened it looking for Ahmad's landline telephone number which he eventually found. He picked up the receiver and started dialling

"Ahmad...Ahmad," said Ed loudly " 0..4..2...3..5...6...6...9" Ed was pronouncing every number slowly then continued dialling "3..3..9" . He then suspected he might have pressed the wrong button numbers so he repeated the number again in a loud voice "Ahmad...0..4...2..3...5..6..6...9...3..3..9"

The phone was ringing on Ahmad's end. Then Ahmad picked up the telephone

"Ahmad.... Hello, Ahmad".

As Ed was speaking he heard a voice saying "04235669339". Ed switched off and did not hear what Ahmad was saying on the other side of the line.

"Ahmad sorry..." said Ed, but he heard the same voice saying the numbers "04235669339"

Ed then looked at the parrot and realised it was the parrot which was repeating these numbers. He smiled and continued his conversation with Ahmad

"Hi Ahmad"

As soon as Ed said "Ahmad", the parrot said the same number "04235669339".

"I shall talk to you later," Ed said to Ahmad and put the receiver down. Ed then moved near the parrot's cage and stared at the parrot with an astonished smile on his face and said "Ahmad". As soon as he finished saying "Ahmad" he heard Ahmad's telephone number pronounced by the parrot "04235669339". Ed then rushed to the parrot and stroked the back of its head and gave it a treat of some crushed fruit, which the parrot enjoyed eating. After few minutes of watching the parrot Ed again said "Ahmad" and the same thing happened again when the parrot repeated Ahmad's telephone number. This immediately was followed again by Ed stroking the head of the parrot. Ed then realised that that type of cognition with the parrot was a new discovery to him and a useful achievement.

"I wonder if I can train this parrot to be a telephone directory! I just have to try," said Ed shaking his head in surprise "It will be a good idea but it's a pity I don't have enough time to make a full use of this ability".

Ed phoned Ahmad again. When Ahmad replied, Ed started a conversation

"Hi Ahmad. Are you OK?" said Ed

"Yes, I am fine, thanks. What are you doing today?" replied Ahmad

"I might stay at home doing some work. Or better I might start my house hunting again," said Ed

"Why don't you come round tonight for a dinner with us? Claire will be cooking a nice Arabic dish and the dolma which you fancy," said Ahmad

"Yeah! That will be fine. Just because of the dolma. How is your daughter?"

"She is fine. We are going out now but will expect you at seven o'clock this evening" said Ahmad happily

"Yes, Ahmad. If you don't mind I have a few things to discuss with you regarding the recent plans for Brazil," said Ed "I am also wondering if you can take over as Head of the Planning Team for four weeks because I am planning to take a holiday"

"Wonderful. You haven't had a holiday for a long time. Of course I will be delighted to test my expertise and learn some leadership skills in your absence. Are you going anywhere exciting?" said Ahmad

"Yes, a very exciting place...in my flat. I just want to relax, but will be in contact with you guys. We can have frequent meetings if necessary. I am not going to isolate myself completely from the company. It's not in anybody's interest if I do that," said Ed.

Ed felt happy when Ahmad agreed to offer his help and support during his absence. Now he had one more task to do; to ask Mr John Basing the Chairman of the company, for a holiday. He remembered the conversation with the Energy Secretary and considered what he said in depth. Ed realised that he was under any obligation to accept what was discussed. He had to find ways in order to release some of his responsibilities and commitments in the company.

When Ed approached Mr Basing asking for four weeks of holiday to have some rest from the routine and do his house hunting, Mr Basing was reluctant in the beginning. However he eventually agreed after obtaining the assurance that Ed would maintain his contact with the company in order to avoid any interruption in services. Mr Basing thought Ed would need some time off work in order to relax and avoid the extra stress within the company. Now that Ed was comfortable in obtaining a period of four weeks' holiday he decided to accept the offer of the Energy Secretary although he felt he was "forced" to accept it in a rather diplomatic and polite way. Ed was ready to meet with the Energy Secretary on Saturday as pre-arranged. On Friday morning Ed received a confirmation phone call from his PA Mrs Emma Jackson to fix the breakfast meeting with the Energy Secretary Mr William Davies. As anticipated the same two men rang his door bell at 10.00 am on the Saturday. Ed had already dressed in his suit. He opened the door, took his laptop with him and accompanied the two men to the Department of Energy. He was welcomed by Mr Davies, who immediately accompanied him to the meeting room where the breakfast was set up ready. Ed and Mr Davies took their seats and began to have the breakfast

"I am very glad to see you again, Sir Edward."

"I am glad too, Mr Davies"

"A nice sunny morning makes a change in one's mood"

"For me, whether it is sunny or cloudy or raining do not make any difference and will not affect me at all. We need the rain as much as we need the sun. There are countries on this planet which dream of having a drop of rain"

"That is very true. I am impressed by your philosophy of life"

"It is not a philosophy. It's reality. Changing weather or being cloudy or rainy has never affected me; if it did I wouldn't have been able to achieve any progress in my life"

"Your policy should stand out as a parable for all the others to follow. No wonder you were knighted. Have you had some thoughts about the discussion we had last week?"

"Yes, I have"

"And...What is the verdict?"

"Before I say yes, which I will, I need to know the scope of the work"

"You made my day, Sir Edward. The Prime Minister will be very pleased to hear that. In fact he will have the pleasure of meeting up with you at number 10, once we have had the full discussion and the final agreement"

"I managed to obtain, though with some difficulty, four weeks of holiday from work when I shall concentrate on your work. If it is not completed I shall see what I can do afterwards"

"I don't think four weeks will be enough. To be honest with you, even double that period won't be enough"

"Mr Davies. Please don't underestimate my ability. We will see. Can you provide me with some more information about the project?"

"I will when we have finished breakfast and moved to my office. You live in a flat don't you?"

"Yes I do"

"Is there any plan to move to a house?"

"Yes, but I don't have enough time for house hunting. It is a co-incidence that you mentioned this because I am planning to view a few houses today"

"Which area are you looking for?"

"Around Slough near to my company"

"Yes. Ensure you purchase a detached house please"

"Why is that? This may be beyond my financial capability"

"This is important for security reason. Once you start the project we shall have to provide 24-hour security to your residence; of course without being noticed by yourself or others. Also the house must be secured with CCTV etcetera. We shall provide that"

"What about the purchase price?"

"Once you sign the contract you will be paid an upfront lump sum which will provide some help. I am certain that will support your deposit for the purchase"

"That will be good"

"Security is the most important issue that matters here. You have only one friend called Ahmad I believe"

"Yes indeed. He is my only friend and also a workmate. He is my deputy at work and will take over much of the work when I am on holiday"

"I don't think there is any concern or issue about Ahmad. However it is essential that you move to your new house before you can start the project in order to ensure that security is in place"

"I shall therefore start my holiday when I am in my new house"

"And after the security measures have completed. But that won't take long. Please ensure you inform me of the address of the property which you want to purchase before any further procedure in the purchasing process is undertaken. This is because we must ensure an initial security check is made on the street, the neighbourhood etcetera"

After finishing breakfast, Mr Davies and Ed moved to Mr Davies' office where they sat round a meeting table which had four surrounding chairs. Mr Davies directed his PA to keep the doors closed and ensure there was no interruption. Mr Davies then started a conversation

"Sir Edward. Again I am very pleased that you kindly agreed to offer your valuable time to act on this project. You will be the sole architectural engineer and we know that you can do the structural engineering calculations"

"But I might have to ask for assistance on the structure. What is this project?"

"Briefly if this project is met with success, it will reduce the cost of the energy supply to the British public substantially"

"I wish my mother was alive to benefit from this project. Poor lady she had to cope with the cost of energy at the time when she was a single mother after the death of my father. She had to work hard to provide me with the necessary standard of living"

"My parents were probably in the same situation too"

"However this is history but I would love to contribute to the improvement of the life of future generations. This will be to ensure their wellbeing and a good standard of living at a cheaper rate. I shall work on this from the bottom of my heart not just for the money but for humanitarian reasons"

"I am impressed by your standards and philosophy in life, Sir Edward. We are confident that you are the best candidate to act as the architect on this project. This is because of many reasons; your ability and your circumstances in addition to your enthusiasm and positive attitude. Of course you will be acting not mainly for the remuneration but also as a project which will make the United Kingdom not just top amongst the European nation but also in the world"

Ed was nodding his head in agreement with the views of Mr Davies who continued

"We are certain and highly value your loyalty to the United Kingdom which is a major reason for our choosing you to play a key role in this project," said Mr Davies going to open a highly secured cupboard to get some papers and plans, which he placed on the table. "Sir Edward. This is a project which is briefly based on providing electricity at a very low cost, firstly to the British population, then we aim to export to the rest of Europe. It utilises all the basic natural products and resources to produce electrical energy. These are refuse, the wind and the sun. In the UK we have an enormous amount of refuse which we get rid of in so many ways. Probably some of these methods may not be environmentally friendly, or even we dump the refuse. Here in this project we aim to burn them; re-use them in a turbo and produce energy. Secondly we shall build windmills which will aid to the process. Thirdly and most importantly, we shall use the sun, which is the best source of energy"

"But we don't have enough sunshine in the UK especially in the winter"

"I knew you would raise this question. This has been dealt with by our physicists and scientists who produced a rather complicated way to acquire the energy from the sun during the periods when the sun is out and store the energy in order to utilise it at time when the sun is not out"

"That seems very interesting and clever"

"Interesting to scientists and physicists but it will be valuable to the country. It will improve the life of the British people by having electricity at a low cost and will improve the economy of the UK when we start selling electricity to Europe"

"I shall need to spend time to study the project to understand the mechanisms and the processes involved"

"Certainly"

"I suppose you will want me to design the buildings which will accommodate all these projects"

"You hit the nail on the head"

Ed took a few minutes looking at the plans and the papers then he said

"I need plenty of time in order to understand these processes and the plans before I make up my mind"

"Make up your mind about what? I thought you had already agreed"

"I am sorry, Mr Davies, perhaps I did not make myself clear. I meant before I make up my mind on how to implement the plans. I need sufficient time to grasp the whole idea. I shall also have to meet your scientists and other teams involved in the ideas. Incidentally are they trust worthy?"

"Rest assured they all are. At this primary stage, these sketches and the project details are all in my office here. You are welcome to spend a few Saturdays here to go through them"

"Can you arrange for those who originated the project to be here next Saturday so that I can meet with them? The best thing is if they come at midday and I shall spend three hours from 9 o'clock to study these before I meet with them"

"That sounds good"

"In the interim I shall continue my house hunting"

"While you are here, my PA will have issued an offer letter to you to act on the project. A contract is ready also for you to inspect before you go. Later we can discuss the remuneration for your professional services"

"Have you chosen the site?"

"Yes, of course. It will be somewhere in Cornwall"

"I shall have to visit the site in three or four weeks' time"

"That is important and will be arranged when you are ready"

"What is the reason behind making it highly secured and secret?"

"Two things matter. One is a possible terrorist activity from various sources aiming to destroy the project. However, most important is the fear of someone creating a similar project elsewhere if any country or organisation becomes aware of the plans, the ideas and the principle. We want this project to be a source of British pride"

"I understand. Mr Davies, I shall see you at 9 o'clock on the morning of next Saturday here as agreed"

Ed received an offer letter from Mrs Jackson, who also gave him a draft contract which he discussed with Mr Davies and suggested some amendments. The contract was signed by both parties after being amended.

Ed went back to his flat. As soon as he entered he made his way to the parrot and shouted "Ahmad". Immediately the parrot mentioned Ahmad's telephone number. Ed brought the parrot a treat of crushed fruit and nuts and stroked the back of its neck and head.

"I must train this parrot on some other telephone numbers or may be other things. I didn't realise it was so useful. At least it keeps me company," said Ed.

Ed was excited about the project and looked forward to his involvement in it. He started making some provisional plans in his head. He spent some time thinking of how the complex should be built so as to preserve its security. He believed that if the building were exposed to public view it would become an easy target despite the security measures which might be imposed and implemented. He concluded that the best step at that time and before any decision or plans were made was to visit the proposed site. He telephoned Mr Davies and asked him to arrange a site visit during the weekend perhaps on the Sunday; the day after his meeting with the group of the scientists involved in the project. In the interim he spent most of his day on Saturday and on Sunday looking for a suitable house to move to.

On the next Saturday, he was accompanied by the same two men to the Energy Department where Mr Davies was waiting for him. He sat down in an office and studied all the proposals and the documents in detail. At mid-day he had a meeting with Mr Davies and the scientists. Ed was able to obtain plenty of information about the project, which he called "an amazing project".

"It seems to be worth spending time to make plans for the building," said Ed to Mr Davies "I am looking forwards to visiting the site tomorrow, as is necessary. However I am thinking if we were planning to employ a substantial number of employees, how can we ensure that those employees will preserve the secret of the project and none of them may be approached by any external organisation, another country or a terrorist organisation with bribery?"

Mr Davies considered what Ed had said seriously. Mr Davies sighed and looked down for a while then raised his head towards Ed. He felt embarrassed in his position as an Energy Secretary that he had proposed such a major national project without paying prior attention to that important matter. When he realised the critical situation, he immediately answered:

"Yes, of course I am aware of this. I am glad that someone of such calibre as yourself is sharing my views and thoughts. That is why I am asking you personally to look into all those matters"

"Mr Davies. I think you are forgetting that I am only an architect. I am not a security expert"

"Sir Edward, you are more than an architect" said Mr Davies with a patently encouraging smile on his face "Basically you were a biomedical scientist. We were able to evaluate you from the point of view of your designs, plans, and thoughts etcetera. The comments and ideas which you always come up with in the newspapers and on television and radio are good evidence of what you are. I don't think you should under-estimate your ability".

"So I understand you want me to give some thought about this aspect. Don't you?"

"You answered the question, Sir Edward. I am not urging you to resolve this matter but I am certain that you will give special consideration to this aspect. Ultimately the plan must consider security as a first prerequisite. Of course all our security experts will be in full co-operation with you in order to... I don't want to say in order to resolve this issue but ...to consider it, or to offer the help which you will need"

There was a period of silence when it seemed that Mr Davies was waiting for an answer from Ed. He was hoping that Ed would be able to resolve this issue since he mentioned it himself. At the same time, Ed was thinking with a deep sigh, staring to one side while Mr Davies kept staring at Ed. Then Ed raised his left forearm while resting his left elbow on the edge of his armchair and put his left thumb on his left cheek and his index and middle finger on his lips, then moved them to his right cheek while still staring to one side. Mr Davies was waiting impatiently for an answer. Then Ed gave a sigh then swallowed and said

"It is something worth considering. I must see the site before making any further comments"

Mr Davies gave a sigh followed by a smile "I am glad you are at least considering this issue"

"But it's not so easy as you may realise," said Ed "That is not a failure of my contract," said ED with a smile as he waited for a reply from Mr Davies

"You may submit a separate invoice for this service. This is in your contract which states you will be remunerated for any additional services which you may provide"

"Mr Davies. The issue is not just remuneration. It's far beyond that. This is such a critical issue and it will not be within my capacity as an architect. Of course I shall consider including some security considerations as far as the plan is concerned"

Mr Davies ceased to smile and stared at Ed sideways anticipating that more would to be said Ed soon realised that Mr Davies wanted assurances about this matter

"I shall try; Mr Davies. I shall try my best," said Ed "But I need to visit the site tomorrow"

Mr Davies had a broad smile on his face. He was certain that Ed would be considering many other issues and not just architectural plans. He was extremely happy that that issue was considered seriously by Ed.

"Sir Edward. Did you have any luck with your house hunt?" asked Mr Davies

"I am going to view a few houses in the evening during the next week!

"As I said, you can start making the plans only when you have moved to your new accommodation. Moving soon will be ideal and serves our purpose. I wait to hear from you"

Ed went back home in the evening planning to give some serious thought to all the issues discussed that day with the scientists but most importantly with Mr Davies. The issues to be considered and taken into account when making the plans were

1. The shape, size site of the buildings. A few environmental issues would have to be considered, speed of the wind, the sun and the smoke from the burning refuse

2. The employees. Their residence. Would it be necessary to build up a large complex to house all the employees and their families or let them live in their own accommodation? If the former was favoured then the issue of security would be great because the residential buildings would be known to the public. While in the latter case, an employee would have to disclose information about his/her employment to the mortgage lender. Additionally, families of the employees would be aware of their relatives' nature of employment and the place of their work.

3. Recruitment of the employees would have to be conducted in such a way as not to breach security

Although Ed's responsibility did not extend to the above issues he was seriously considering them. He thought that those issues were to be discussed in a meeting with the rest of the top personnel concerned. Ed realised that the whole project was rather more complicated than he originally believed. However he did not regret his decision to be involved because he liked challenges.

When Ed arrived home, he heard the parrot saying "Good evening". Ed went to the parrot and said "Good evening". The parrot then said "How are you?". Ed's response was "Fine, thank you". Ed gave the parrot a big smile and went to the kitchen to make it some crushed fruits and nuts and brought them to its cage then filled the water cup and placed in the cage too. Ed then practised the parrot's ability to memorise some telephone numbers which he trained the parrot on. He was pleased to see the parrot remembering those numbers when he mentioned the name of the person as a cue. Ed also realised that in order for the parrot to act as a directory for any issue it would have to be trained continuously for a few days. The other major issue was his house hunting which Ed had to finalise and move to the new accommodation quickly in order to be enabled to start planning for the project.

On the next day, Sunday, Ed and the Energy Secretary accompanied by some of the scientists involved and security personnel took a trip to Cornwall to visit the site. It was a huge rural setting near the sea. Sir Edward spent a few hours there and took a few photographs. He returned home with more enthusiasm than before.

Ed viewed a few properties during the week and managed to choose a few houses which he informed Mr Davies of. Immediately steps were taken by the security personnel and at the end of the week one of the houses was recommended for Ed to purchase. The process of the purchase began and within two months Ed completed the purchasing process and moved into his house. He took the parrot with him and placed the cage in the sitting room. Soon after moving, a CCTV system was installed by the order of the Energy Secretary and security surveillance was in place.

Ed began his four weeks of holiday to allow him to work on the plans for the big project. During the period of planning he often had to contact the scientists with whom he had a few meetings. He also had a few meetings with Mr Davies.

~Chapter 6~

Kate

Towards the end of the second week of his holiday which Ed spent working on the project plans in his new house, he felt his eyes becoming tired. He found them red and watery when he looked in the mirror. The eyes were itching continuously; a symptom which caused Ed frequent interruptions to his work. He found those symptoms annoying and stressful. Owing to time constraint, he decided to deal with that issue as quickly as a possible. Because Ed was covered by health insurance by his company he was able to obtain an appointment to see a consultant ophthalmologist, Miss Kate Fernandes, privately soon. Ed entered the consulting room and he saw the good-looking ophthalmologist with long black hair, fair skin, thin figure, nicely dressed and with lightly made up wide eyes. She was 175 cm height, slightly taller than Ed, who was 172cm in height. She welcomed him

"Hello, Sir Edward. Please have a seat"

He sat down on the chair

"Thank you, Miss Fernandes"

"Aren't you Sir Edward James Carpenter, the famous architect?"

"I don't like to be addressed as a famous person. Much as I am needed in the society, you are more in need. We need a street sweeper as much we need an architect," said Ed in a very quiet and humble manner

"I am not just talking to a famous architect. It seems I am talking to a very humble and modest man"

"Miss Fernandes. I regard myself as a servant to the people, to the nation and to society"

Miss Fernandes was nodding her head with every word Ed was saying and looking impressed. Then she looked at the notes on her desk

"I see you are 42 years old," silent for 4 seconds, "and a Sir?! You must have been very busy and active and God knows what you had achieved in order to be knighted"

"I share all your views." She looked at his notes again "Do you realise we were both born in January, but not on the same day or the same year?"

"Still Capricorn"

"Quite"

"They say Capricorn people are clever"

"Everyone is clever in a certain way but it depends how this is utilised"

"There is a lot to learn from you. What is your marital status?

"I am single"

"Anyway, what is the problem?"

"It's my eyes which have been itching and hurting. I also noticed they were red"

"How long have you had these symptoms for?"

"A week, but the symptoms are interfering with my job. I have a project which I have to complete in two weeks and I will not be able to if I am still like this. I need your help"

"Has there been any change in your environment?"

"Yes I moved house. I used to live in a flat but moved about a month ago to my current address"

"Do you have a garden?"

"Yes a big one"

"Do you spend some time in the garden?"

"Yes when I have a little break"

"Do you have a pet?"

"A parrot"

"A parrot? How interesting. Rarely do people get a parrot"

"Because they don't realise what they are missing. Any way if you think my condition may be linked to the parrot, I don't think so because I have had it for a few months now"

"Let me have a look at your eyes," said Miss Fernandes. She then stood up and came to Ed and looked at his eyes holding his head with her soft fingers. She examined both eyes.

"I am going to put in some drops which will dilate the pupils in order to examine the inside of your eyes clearly by the slit lamp," said Miss Fernandes. Then she put one drop into each eye and waited for few minutes.

"Your surname must be Portuguese," commented Ed

"Yes it is my dad's surname. He is from Lisbon"

"Lisboa, as it is called"

"Correct"

"Lots of female doctors continue using their maiden name and do not use their marital name"

"I am not married. I think I can now examine your eyes by the slit lamp"

Miss Fernandes examined him by the slit lamp.

"How is your eye sight? Do you wear glasses?"

"I don't wear glasses. I have good eye sight. I think"

"There is nothing significant. Your retina and the lenses are perfect. You have some form of conjunctivitis which is an allergy especially at this time of year. May be when you moved to your house you were exposed to pollens. Additionally stress and lack of sleep may contribute. Do you get enough sleep?"

"You hit the nail on the head. I didn't get enough hours of sleep in the last two weeks. I have been very busy"

"Your eyes need some rest. I am going to prescribe some eye drops which you use four times daily then I shall review you in two weeks," said Miss Fernandes. She gave Ed her personal card "Here is my card with my personal mobile telephone number. Please feel free to call me any time when you need me"

"Thank you very much, Miss Fernandes." He took the prescription and shook hands with Miss Fernandes "I will see you in two weeks"

"Earlier if you so wish. My secretary will arrange the appointment"

Ed left Miss Fernandes mumbling to himself "She was so soft and nice, a good-looking lady. Good personality".

Ed used his drops for one week while working on the plans. He made the arrangement to have a meeting with the Energy Secretary on the Saturday. However, on the Friday evening his mobile telephone rang with a number which was not known to him

"Hello"

"Sir Edward Carpenter?"

"Yes"

"It is Kate Fernandes"

"Hello, Miss Fernandes"

"I am phoning to see how you are"

"Great. I think you had the magic touch on my eyes and my body as a whole"

"Does this mean you are better?"

"Better? I am cured"

"Wonderful news, Sir Edward. I am very pleased"

"However I am still suffering from lack of sleep. I think the lack of sleep will continue for the next two or three weeks then hopefully will be OK"

"I think it was an allergy which you had. However you have to pay attention to your health and get relaxed"

"I am supposed to be on holiday now"

"You're joking!"

"I am telling you the truth. Believe me. I am now busier than if I were at work"

"Why is that?"

"I was asked to do a project which I could not do except if I had a holiday"

"You are impossible"

"What makes life easy now is I am alone as always"

"Not even a friend?"

"Well. I have only one friend who is a workmate, but I am not going to see him except when I go back to work because I am rather busy with what I am doing. I am crying for time"

"I also have one friend only"

"He must be a doctor too"

"It's a she. Strangely she is not a doctor. I am sorry I have taken so much of your time. I phoned only to ask you about your eyes"

"Not at all please; I enjoyed talking to you"

"I enjoyed too. I don't know why"

"Probably because we are both Capricorn"

"Yes, you reminded me of that"

"It's a strange co-incidence"

"OK I'll let you go and enjoy the rest of your evening with your work"

"I am seeing you next week for a review"

"I look forward to it"

"I do too"

"Goodbye for now"

"Goodbye, Miss Fernandes"

After putting the receiver down, Ed kept holding it in its place, staring forwards with a mild smile on his face. He then mumbled to himself

"What an attractive soft voice over the phone she had. It ties in very well with how she looks. Her boyfriend is lucky!" He then was silent for five seconds "But she said she doesn't have a friend except one female friend. I wonder if she is a.....you never know...." He turned his face to the parrot " I tell you my friend; she is so beautiful.... beautiful. She has black hair, big wide eyes...slightly taller than me but probably she was wearing high-heeled shoes. Her voice is so soft and feminine. What do you think, my dear Mister Parrot? You are silent so you are in agreement. Do you know what her name is? Kate. Remember Kate" He went nearer to the parrot and said Kate a few times. Ed was silent for a while thinking of Miss Fernandes "Any way I must prepare for my meeting with the Energy Secretary tomorrow". He then left the sitting room to get a few more papers. Then he heard the parrot saying "Kate" a few times. He immediately brought it some chocolates and put them in the cage

"Here we are, Mister Parrot. Some treats for you. Keep reminding me of Kate. Kate"

On the next day, Saturday, Ed was at a long meeting with Mr Davies showing him the preliminary plans

"Mr Davies. I think it is the best option to have the whole plant under the ground, which will make it highly secure and not approachable. The entrance will be highly secured and there will be a long approach which will go round and round in circle till you reach the plant. I made provisions for ventilation, recreation facilities, a swimming pool and even a large area where there is a skylight."

"But the sky light can be detected from the top...I mean from the ground level"

"Not actually. Firstly most of it will be deep under the ground level where there will be a huge open car park and a playground on the top of it. Over the rest of it and next to the car park, there will be a large shopping mall for the public. Accordingly, no one will suspect what is underneath. The sky light will go through the shopping mall to the top and people will think it's part of the shopping centre because the glass will be obscured, not see-through. The entrance to the plant which will be secured of course and gated will appear to the public as if it is an entrance to a staff car park. There will be security at a few levels of the approach road to enter the plant"

"This is genius. It is a genius plan. This is why we chose you to do it"

"The shopping mall will be the largest in the whole region and will be a multi-storey centre. There is a reason; in fact a very important reason, why it's a multi-storey"

Mr Davies kept looking at the drawings opening his mouth in surprise at the whole plan

"Why?" said Mr Davies

"So that the chimney stands up through it and is unnoticeable although most of the smoke will be re-used inside the plant to work the turbos. Hence the amount of the smoke coming out will be negligible"

"Fantastic. Really fantastic. I am certain the Prime Minister will be very pleased with this"

"Give the Prime Minister my regards when you see him"

"He would love to meet you. Incidentally what about the employees' commitments to be loyal to the project and avoid exposing the secrets or the address to others"

"Mr Davies. This is beyond my capacity. However, I thought of one way but I don't know how ethical and legal it is. It's just a thought. I don't want to be quoted on it and I shall not put it in black and white"

"Can you kindly explain?"

"Every employee is to be hypnotised before joining the company. The hypnosis condition can be made a clause in the contract; hence you will be covered legally. As I said, it's just an idea"

"Can you please explain?"

"During hypnosis each employee will be told to reject any offer of being contacted by other organisations or countries which try to steal the ideas of this plant and to reject any bribery or gifts. As I said it's just a thought"

"I don't know how we can go about it. How does hypnosis work?"

"The suggestions which you give to the employee are supposed to go through to the subconscious mind and be embedded there"

"I don't think we shall need this approach but we have to agree with our security services on certain ways to secure loyalty to the project"

"I am glad you can think about this in a different way. Are you happy with the plans so far?"

"Yes of course"

"The next thing will be to meet with the scientists and make another site visit. After that I shall produce the final plans. Once these are approved we shall work on the structural side and do the calculations"

"Are you happy in your new house?"

"I am indeed. It's so quiet and that is what I need"

"Perfect"

"Can I go now?"

"Yes of course. When will we meet again?

"I shall be meeting the scientists tomorrow followed by a site visit, How about next Saturday for the final draft? My holiday will be over by then and I shall go back to work in the week after"

Ed left Mr Davies and went home. When he entered his sitting room he heard the parrot saying "Kate" repeatedly. He smiled and went to it to say

"Aah Mr Parrot, you don't know how beautiful she is. Please keep reminding me of her"

Ed had a meeting with the scientists as planned then went with them on a site visit. He came back home to do the final draft of the plans ready for his meeting with the Energy secretary on Saturday.

On Thursday Ed went for his appointment to see Miss Fernandes in her private consulting room. He bought her an expensive chocolate collection and a valuable necklace. He entered the consulting room to say after a warm welcome from Miss Fernandes

"Miss Fernandes I hope you will like these simple gifts"

"Wow Sir Edward! I don't deserve all this. Why is that? I didn't do more than what I do to others and any way I am paid for it by the insurance company"

"Miss Fernandes. You deserve more than this. What you have done to me was amazing. It changed my life. I can now do my work perfectly and without any problem. Without you I might have been a blind person by now!"

"Not blind! It wasn't anything more than allergic conjunctivitis which responded to simple treatment"

"To you it was simple but to me it was life-saving. I owe you a lot Miss Fernandes"

"You owe me nothing"

"Miss Fernandes. I want to say something but I hope you do not disappoint me"

"My pleasure is if it is within my capacity"

"I promise it will not exceed that"

"OK Carry on Sir Edward"

"I am inviting you for dinner on Saturday evening. Will you accept?"

"I am more than delighted, Sir Edward. How can I reject this invitation from the famous Sir Edward Carpenter?"

"I am more delighted Miss Fernandes than you are"

"I look forwards to Saturday evening"

"I shall choose somewhere which is close to both of us. Where do you live Miss Fernandes?"

"In Gerard's Cross"

"That is great. It's not far from where I in live Slough. I shall phone you about the place and if you don't mind I shall come to pick you up"

"Agreed with great pleasure"

Ed then left the office of Miss Fernandes full of joy and happiness that she accepted his invitation to join him for dinner. Ed had never had any relation previously with any female. In addition to being dyslexic, Ed was shy in his life and reserved. He didn't have friends whether men or women except for Ahmad, whom he had known for the previous 15 years. Ed now began to realise that he needed a female partner. He began to realise that life without a female was boring. At home, the only one that he talked to was the parrot which he came to know only recently. But again he thought about it and did not want to put all his hopes on Miss Fernandes because his knowledge about her was next to nil. Equally she knew no more than what a doctor ought to know about a patient in one or two consultations.

Kate Fernandes on the other hand was surprised by the invitation from Ed. In her life this was the first invitation from a patient. She could not reject an invitation from an important person like Sir Edward Carpenter, the famous architect. She was thrilled by this invitation which she was not expecting. As a person, she found Ed interesting ad handsome with a very good character. He shared with her a few views in addition to the month she was born in. However, she did not share with him the same emotional feelings which he had towards her. What surprised Kate, was the highly valuable gift which he brought her.

Ed had his meeting with the Energy Secretary on Saturday morning to complete the final draft of the plans. Mr Davies approved the plans and told Ed that this would be subject to the Prime Minister's and the Cabinet's approval.

"The security of keeping these plans is the most crucial matter in this whole project as explained previously. If we keep those documents in our possession even in a secured place then we don't know where the responsibility will fall if something happens. I mean if it gets known to some organisations who are interested in such plans or other countries. The worst would be if it falls in the hands of terrorists," said Mr Davies

"And what does this mean?" asked Ed

"Both the Prime Minister and I thought that the best interests of the nation, the plans should be be left with one person to look after and keep them in his possession. We thought that this person should be someone who does not attract any suspicion that he might possess that information."

"Correct. This is a good idea"

"I am glad that you share this view with us"

"Good. You may be the one, Mr Davies"

"This is not the right choice. Not even the Prime Minister"

"Why is that? You know everything about the plans and the project"

"OK what happens if our party loses the general election next year? I shall be probably a back bencher if I am lucky enough to be elected to the House of Commons"

"Yes. That is a good point. I am not a politician so I don't think along those lines"

"Hence our decision was to choose someone who will not attract attention from any external source. This person should not be a politician, a member of our security services or a member of the Cabinet"

"Good thoughts"

"Therefore the choice will be the one and only one person who will not be suspected of holding this information"

"Good choice"

"It's a good choice if you know whom I mean"

There was silence for a few seconds while Ed was waiting for Mr Davies to name the person he was talking about.

"The person chosen to be the sole one to keep those highly secret documents is...." Mr Davies stared at Ed for a while "Is ...You, Sir Edward"

Ed raised his eyes and stared at Mr Davies

"Do you mean...me!?" said Ed with surprise

"Yes..You," nodding his head "Don't you want to be holding the top secret document in the interests of the people, economy and national security of the United Kingdom?"

"I could have thought of any person on this planet but not me" Ed said after a deep sigh "I work in a company in which I carry a huge responsibility. It will therefore be next to impossible for me to be responsible for such a task"

"I am afraid there is no other choice. Firstly no one will be aware that you have made those plans. This is why we chose you in person rather than giving this task to your company. Secondly you are a very reserved single person and have only one friend in your life so no one at all will be suspicious of you. The situation would be much different if it was in our hands"

"I am now a single person. What will happen if I get married tomorrow?"

"No problem. Now that you have finished the task you can go and get married and do whatever suits you. No objection but of course we anticipate your wife or your partner should not be made aware of this"

"OK Can I think about it?"

"Yes you can think about it but I can tell you what we anticipate the answer has to be, yes, I am afraid, Sir Edward," said Mr Davies with a mild smile on his face

"So there is no need to waste time in thinking about it"

"My advice is yes, there is no need to waste your time thinking about it. Sir Edward; do you realise how important your holding of the information is to the United Kingdom? I am sure one day history will record this particular task which you fulfilled"

Ed gave another sigh and lowered his head down, then swallowed

"Sir Edward. You will also be greatly remunerated for this task which is in the interest of the national security plus any cost incurred," said Mr Davies "Are you happy now?"

Ed stared sideway at Mr Davies and said after few seconds of silence

"Happy and not happy. I am happy because I am responsible for such an important task and not happy because it's a responsibility which is beyond my ability. I am only an architect"

"Sir Edward. As I said please do not underestimate your value and capability for the United Kingdom"

"OK Mr Davies. I must now go and think of ways to perform this task and store all this information"

"Sir Edward. Remember. Storing it on a computer is not a good idea at all. A computer may get crushed, stolen or hacked"

"I understand that. I do understand"

"Good luck. Please keep me informed. Please work on the structural calculations and keep me posted"

"OK, Mr Davies," said Ed, then stood up to go with a gloomy face and signs of unhappiness.

Ed left the office. While on his way, Ed was thinking of how he was going to store all the plans and the information safely and beyond the reach of any person. He was glad he was living alone and was not in a relationship. He arrived home and as a usual routine he went to the parrot and said "Hello Mr Parrot. How are you today?"

The parrot replied "Kate" repeatedly. Ed smiled but then said "Listen, Parroty. There is a new task laid on me today. I think you should help me. I think you could help me".

The response of the parrot was to say "Kate" repeatedly.

Ed at this time did not think about the project, but he was thinking of the dinner he was going to have with Kate in the evening. He went out to do his usual walking exercise and shopping. He then went out again to buy a bottle of perfume for Kate. He phoned Kate

"Hello Miss Fernandes"

"Is that Sir Edward?"

"Yes, it is"

"I was thinking of you. I was waiting for your phone call"

Ed sighed with a big smile on his face. There was a happy silence. But as Kate was waiting for a reply, she said

"Hello. Are you there?"

"Yes.. yes, Miss Fernandes. Your words made my day"

"Really? To that extent?"

"Please make your choice. Do you fancy an Indian restaurant, Italian, Middle Eastern, Persian or any other restaurant?"

"I have never tried Middle Eastern or Persian restaurants before"

"OK. Leave it with me. I shall come to pick you up at..." He looked at the wall clock then continued " at 7 o'clock. Does this suit you?

"It is perfect. I look forward to seeing you"

"Please text me your full address and the post code"

"Will do straight away"

"Bye for now"

He was very happy with this conversation. For the first time in his life he felt emotional. A lady was entering his heart. However, he was still sceptical; he did not want to advance any further in his emotions in the event of disappointment if Kate did not feel as he did. Ed was aware that he was shy and reserved; therefore those two "negative" traits, as he believed, might not be helpful in placing him in the heart of a lady like Kate. He didn't know Kate's age but from the way she looked, behaved and from her profession as a consultant she would be of an age close to his or a few years younger. Hence this might mean they were matched in thoughts and ideas. Therefore he wasn't totally enthusiastic but he aimed at playing his game and exploring further.

Ed dressed nicely. He put on the best of his ties and wore an aftershave. He took the perfume gift he purchased for Kate and left home in his modest car. Luck played its game when there was a big traffic jam as a result of an accident on his way to Gerard's Cross. This made him nervous. He managed to pull up his car on the side of the road and phoned Kate to inform her he would be a little late. Eventually he arrived 45 minutes late. Kate's house was a detached house with a driveway to parking in the front garden. Ed phoned Kate to inform her he was waiting outside her front door. Kate then opened the door and came out dressed up in a very attractive dress with light makeup. When Ed saw her coming out he stepped out of his car and shook hand with her. He found himself unable to resist staring at the beauty standing in front of him. His eyes were fixed on hers which made her realise he was swimming in the sea of her appearance. She gave him the time he required to satisfy his desire of looking at her with a sufficient period of silence. Kate became aware that Ed was attracted by her but like him, she wasn't certain of his exact intentions; accordingly she didn't show any reaction and decided to act with reserve.

"Good evening madam," said Ed with his hands still gripping Kate's

"Good evening, Sir Edward. It is very nice to see you and thanks for this invitation"

"Not at all. It's the least I could do for...for" said Ed while still staring at her, but he couldn't continue; he was shy.

"Shall we go now? I think we are already late"

Ed realised that he should wake up from his dreams of Kate's beauty and get on with the dinner. "Yes, Miss Fernandes". He soon pulled away his hands while becoming aware his muscles were shaking in puzzlement. He soon went to open the front door for Kate

"Miss Fernandes. Please do sit in my rather modest car"

"A car is important to take you from point A to point B. It doesn't matter what it is as long as it is safe to carry you" She sat in the car and Ed shut the door then went round to open the driver's side door and got in

"What you said is exactly what is in my mind and what I believe. This is another issue that we have our agreement on". He looked at her before starting his car "Miss Fernandes. Please allow me to say one thing before I start the engine" Ed began to sweat and drops of perspiration appeared on his forehead

"Go ahead, please, and say it"

Ed swallowed and kept looking at Kate and realised he couldn't continue what he wanted to say. Kate saw his right hand shaking but she raised her eyes to look at him. He took his shaky right hand from the steering wheel, turned his face to the windscreen and put his right fingers on the car key to start the engine. Soon Ed saw Kate's sweet soft right hand on his right hand touching him swiftly but softly

"Calm down, Sir Edward. You look a bit nervous. What did you want to say?"

Ed stared at her hand then turned his face to her and saw her eyes staring at him as she was aware what he wanted to say but she wanted to hear it from him

"Later, Miss Fernandes. Later. We don't have enough time now"

Kate took her hand off his. Ed started the engine and moved the car. The smell of the perfume she was wearing affected Ed's emotion strongly and added to her attraction. While driving, they had a little conversation about the weather and Gerard's Cross where she had been living for the previous five years. They then talked about the significant rise in house prices. Within 15 minutes they arrived at a Persian restaurant in Slough near his company headquarters. He got out of his car and opened the door for Kate, who stepped out, then Ed shut the door again. They both went in to the restaurant. Kate was impressed by Ed's manner of opening the door for her. They sat down in a quiet corner

"You are most welcome, Miss Fernandes. Please from now on call me Ed"

"And I am Kate. Now tell me what you wanted to say before you started the car?"

Ed stared at her again and as he was about to speak, they heard a voice

"Is that Sir Edward Carpenter?" asked the Restaurant owner, who was dressed in a suit and was standing near Ed and Kate "Yes, it is Sir Edward Carpenter," said Ed raising his face to the man

"How nice, sir to meet you and what a great honour to have you in our restaurant. I am the owner of the restaurant. It will be our great pleasure if you and your wife agree to be our guests tonight"

When Ed heard the owner addressing Kate as his wife he felt the words were entering his ears like music. He didn't comment but looked at Kate to see her reaction. Equally Kate looked at Ed, anticipating that Ed would comment on that assumption. There was silence from both Kate and Ed as each was anticipating a comment from the other.

The restaurant owner proffered his hand to shake Ed's hand.

"Sir Edward. There will be no need for you to order. I shall arrange a variety of our specialities which I hope will be to you and your wife's satisfaction"

"Thanks Sir. This is very kind of you," said Ed. Then he looked at Kate, who was smiling

"Now, sir and madam. What would you like to drink? We have anything you require except for alcohol, which we don't serve here"

"I don't drink alcohol," said Kate

"Can we have that special yogurt drink you make? I don't remember its name"

"Do you mean doogh?"

"Yes. That's it," said Ed then turned his face to Kate "You try it and see if you like it. I think you will"

"I like natural drinks. Yogurt will suit me fine," said Kate

"OK I shall now go and get your dinner ready. You will have the doogh soon and hope you will enjoy our food," said the Restaurant owner. Then he left the couple in peace.

Kate looked at Ed then said

"Did you hear what the owner addressed me as?"

"Yes. Do you have any objection? It wasn't appropriate to deny it. I didn't have the courage to say the opposite"

"But it is not true"

"I know that," said Ed after a sigh

"Now tell me, Sir Edward"

"Ed please"

"Sorry. Ed"

Soon her words were interrupted by a waiter bringing the doogh in a jug. He poured it in the glasses and left the jug on the table.

"Ed. Tell me what you wanted to say when we were in the car before you drove to here"

Ed lowered his head down for few seconds then raised his eyes to her and gave a sigh. He kept looking at her, then swallowed, then lowered his eyes again then raised them to look at Kate again. When Kate heard no answer she started to speak

"Ed. Please tell me what you wanted to say. You look nervous. You seem to be hiding something. Was there something wrong with me or on me that you wanted to comment on?"

Ed stared at her again and a few drops of sweat appeared on his forehead. He was nervous. Soon another waiter came with varieties of starters which he put on the table. Immediately the restaurant owner came back to say

"I hope everything is OK with the starters. Do you have any questions?"

"Thank you very much. I know what these dishes are. I am familiar with Persian food," said Ed

"But I haven't seen you here before. You probably have been to other Persian restaurants. Perhaps you will explain to your wife what these dishes are and save me the time to explain"

"Of course I will," said Ed. The restaurant owner then left

"I am not going to eat," said Kate looking at Ed with a serious face

"Why not? I am sorry. Do you want us to go to another restaurant? I am prepared to do anything to please you," said Ed

"I am not going to start eating until you have told me what you wanted to say"

"Kate," said Ed raising his head to Kate and looking at her "Kate you are.. you are gorgeous"

Kate stared at him with a wide smile as she was waiting for him to continue. Then he continued, "I have never said this to any lady or girl before. Believe me, never. You are the first lady whom I have said this too"

"Probably you said other words to other ladies"

"Not even similar words. Trust me Kate"

"What made you say that?"

"Do you want a true and easy answer?"

"Yes"

"When you go back home...sorry I meant when I take you back home; please stand up against a mirror and you will see the answer yourself when you look in the mirror. I am so sorry, Kate if I over-stepped any boundaries in my conversation with you or toward you. I was only expressing my feelings"

Kate continued staring at him and seemed to be enjoying his description

"Now that you know the answer can you start, please?" said Ed

Kate gave Ed a wide smile while listening to him, then started eating.

"Please help yourself and try every one of these starters. They are lovely," said Ed happily after he had overcome his nervousness and fears of expressing his feelings. On the other hand Kate was so pleased to hear Ed's views about her and within herself she thought that probably Ed's expressions were nothing more than his views and could have been said by any man. However Ed's comments that he had never used such expression to any woman previously made her think about the reason for his expression if he was telling the truth.

"You have a nice large house. Do you live alone?"

"Yes but often my parents and my sister come to visit me from Lisbon. What about you Ed?"

"I am single and live alone with my parrot."

"Do you enjoy that?"

"It's not a matter of enjoying it. Who enjoys living alone between four walls without anyone to talk to? I am beginning to feel the boredom of being alone."

"But you have the parrot to talk to and presumably it talks also"

"I meant I am alone without a human being to communicate with under the same roof"

"So what do you do when you come home in the evening?"

"My work never ends when I come home. Have you been married before?"

"No. What about you? Have you been married?"

"Snap"

"Any partner or friends?"

"Not really, but I have just one workmate friend, called Ahmad. He is married with one child"

"I too, have only one friend, who is a pharmacist. I sometimes meet up with her. I heard you saying you have never passed any comment to a lady. Do you mind if I ask you why?"

"Not at all. I was shy during my upbringing, but that is not the only reason. I have never had the chance to meet someone whom I think I am attached to or who attracts me or she and I are compatible. What about you?"

"I was brought up in a very reserved conservative Catholic family. We don't believe in sex before marriage, for example. Most of the men nowadays won't come near you unless you have sex with them. Subsequently, life goes on until both partners decide to continue as friends, separate or get married. They might stay like this for years. This is something neither my family nor I believe in and which I am not interested in. This has limited my chances of meeting the right person. Of course, there may be another reason though it's trivial as I believe. As a consultant who works both in the National Health Service and in the private sector, I don't have the time for social life. It's so boring"

"I think I am in agreement with you. This is the general attitude which is taken as the norm in life everywhere not just in this country. The reason for our thoughts being along the same lines is probably because we both are mature enough to think positively in life rather than like young teenagers".

"So what is your plan in life after all this progress which you have made and being knighted?"

"Do you mean partner wise?"

"Yes in other ways"

"I am now forty-two as you may know. I hope I find the right partner to get married to and have a family with rather than just for a friendship. I am not young and I also need to establish my social life. I find it difficult sometimes when I come home and see myself alone. Life is boring without a partner at home. What about you?"

"The same if I find the right partner who accepts me in my belief namely no sex before marriage which I shall never give up. I also do not drink alcohol. I may look strange and boring to others but here I am"

The owner of the restaurant arrived again to say

"Is everything OK?"

"Yes, thank you," said Ed

"Is your wife happy? Is the starter OK, madam?"

"It is delicious. I think we should come here frequently, Ed," said Kate

"Yes, of course," said Ed

"I shall now get the main menu ready for you. Enjoy it and let me know should you need anything," said the owner then left them eating

"He seems to be a nice man, Ed"

"Well, we are his guests today. In any case I am at your service and you will be my guest in the future again and again"

"That is very kind of you, Ed"

"At your service, Kate,

and I am very delighted to have your company"

Kate began to enjoy talking to Ed. She understood that Ed was sincere in what he said to her. She felt she was attracted to him. The next steps were to know each other better and in more depth. The main menu was brought. It contained varieties of barbequed lamb and chicken and some rice.

"From whom did you inherit this beauty, Kate? I mean your eyes, your hair everything?"

"I look like my mother. Thank you very much for your compliments, which I think I don't deserve. There are so many beautiful ladies around and I don't think I look as beautiful as others do"

"I am impressed by your modesty. It is not just the colour of the eyes and hair which matters. I believe when there is attraction between a man and a woman that it's not just how you look which matters but it is what is inside your body. It is the soul which creates the attraction between the two genders. This in my belief matters more than external beauty. I say that probably because I am not a teenager or in my early twenties"

"Ed, you talk very nicely. I believe in what you say although I have never had any experience before".

Ed and Kate continued their general conversation. Both had sufficient preliminary information about each other. Kate felt she fancied Ed and Ed felt he loved Kate, but neither of them had the courage or the willingness to express their emotional feelings. Both wanted to allow more time to know each other before making any decision.

They finished dining at 10.30 pm and were making their way to the exit. They wanted to thank the owner of the restaurant who brought the guest book and asked Ed to write his views about the restaurant. Ed held the pen in his left hand and wrote some positive comments about the dining experience and the food, then signed. The restaurant owner eventually shook hand with Ed and said" Bye Sir Edward Carpenter" Then he shook hand with Kate and said, "Bye, Lady Carpenter".

Kate and Ed left the restaurant, sat in the car and Ed drove Kate to her residence. On the way Ed said

"It was good food, wasn't it Kate?"

"Delicious I enjoyed it. This was my first experience of Persian food"

"Next week I am going to take you to a different restaurant"

"That is very kind of you. Do I deserve all that just for a consultation which I am already paid for?"

"That is nothing, but it was not just for your consultation. I have been to see doctors a few times previously but have never taken any one of them out for dinner"

"Why me in particular?"

Ed turned his face for a second to look at her with a smile, then turned his face looking at the windscreen concentrating on his driving and said

"I think by now you are clever enough to know the answer"

"I don't. I would like to hear it from you"

"Did you hear how the restaurant owner was addressing you? Lady Carpenter"

"Yes I did"

"He thought you were my wife"

"You didn't answer my question"

"What question?"

"Are you forgetful?"

"Only sometimes. Especially if I am anaesthetised by beauty. I hope this answers your question"

Kate was pleased to hear the comments from Ed. Her pleasure was conveyed in a noticeable deep smile on her face. There was a silence for a minute, then Ed started to speak

"It is after eleven o'clock"

"Why is that? Do you think we spent too long time in the restaurant?"

"On the contrary. Time has passed so quickly. It felt like one minute only"

They arrived at Kate's house. Ed stopped the car and while he was unfastening his seat belt he heard the click of Kate opening her car door. He immediately put his left hand on her left forearm and said

"No Kate. Please. Let me do my duty". He then opened his door and stepped out. Ed opened the door himself for Kate, who got out of the car.

"Just one second, Kate". Ed opened the left rear door of his car and took out the present he bought for Kate wrapped in a nice gift bag and gave it to Kate

"Kate, I hope you accept this simple gift from me"

"Many thanks, Ed. I don't deserve all that," said Kate after a sigh with a smile on her face

"You deserve more than this. Kate. It's not for you"

"But for whom?" said Kate with a surprised face

"It is for the beauty that you carry" He kept staring at her eyes with nervousness. He felt his heart was beating fast and he was breathing more deeply. Kate was staring at his eyes. Soon Ed said

"It is cold here"

"Perhaps you can come in. Visit my house and see it"

Ed was not surprised by what he heard, but her words made a deep impression on him. Ed could not resist accepting that offer. There was no intention in his mind apart from having a great chance to know Kate better. He gave Kate a large smile and said

"I'll be delighted to" Ed shut the car doors and followed Kate to the door.

Kate opened her handbag to get the keys out. She continued to look for the keys but couldn't find them. She became nervous while Ed was waiting

"Oh! My God!! I must have forgotten the keys inside the house. What an embarrassment"

"Let me see if they didn't fall accidentally on the ground here or perhaps in the car"

"Ed. Please look for them in the car and I shall search this area here".

Ed went to search his car while Kate lit the light of her mobile phone searching the front yard of the house. After a while Ed came and saw Kate standing up as she had finished her search

"Any luck?" asked Kate.

Ed shook his head in disappointment

"What can I do now? I think I must go to a hotel," said Kate

There was a short silence which was broken by the noise of the wind against the leaves.

"Please take me to a local hotel. There is one in Gerard's Cross and one nearby in Denham"

Kate walked to the car, followed by Ed who opened the door for her. She got in. Ed shut her door and went round to open the driver's side door and sat down. He fastened his seat belt, put the key in the ignition but did not switch on the engine. He put both his hands on the steering wheel and bent his head over the wheel as he was thinking

"What's the matter, Ed? Why don't you move?" asked Kate.

Ed turned his head to Kate while keeping his hands on the steering wheel and stared at her

"What's the matter Ed? Are you all right?" asked Kate in surprise

"Why do you want to go to a hotel? We need to talk and I was happy to spend some more time with you at your home"

"So what can I do then?"

"I hope you will not reject my offer"

"What's that?"

"Come and stay in my house. Tomorrow is a Sunday"

"Ed. I am sorry to say. I have never spent the night with a man before. I feel embarrassed and nervous. I can't accept your offer. Sorry"

"But you will have to do it once. Anyway I have four bedrooms and we can sort you out. Trust me," said Ed with a looks of sincerity on his face begging Kate to spend the night at his home "I know my house is modest compared to yours but it will be better than a hotel. It will also save you some money"

Ed said the last sentence with a joking smile on his face

"If it is for the sake of saving few pounds, yes.. go ahead," said Kate jokingly and laughed

"Fantastic. You made my day," said Ed with a deep smile, full of joy.

Ed then started the engine and drove the car towards his residence in Slough. Upon arrival and after parking the car, Ed opened the house door and switched off the burglar alarm then let Kate enter. He switched on the light of the sitting room and the parrot shouted "Hello"

"Who is that?" Kate said in surprise

"Oh..I thought I told you, there is someone living with me at home. My housemate"

"No, you didn't Ed. I am sorry, I can't stay here tonight"

"Calm down. You didn't ask me who this housemate is"

"Who is this housemate of yours?" asked Kate, looking at Ed without blinking her eyes

"The parrot. Look there" He pointed out at the parrot. Kate laughed and walked towards the parrot.

"I am going to make some coffee," said Ed, making his way to the kitchen to make the coffee

"White with no sugar for me please," shouted Kate

"OK Kate, at your service," shouted Ed

Kate walked away from the parrot to put her handbag on the dining table. She then stood up looking around the sitting room which measured about 6X6 metres, with the curtains drawn in front of a bay window. While forming an impression of how tidy Ed was, she heard some words from the parrot. She then stopped and turned her head towards the parrot from a distance and clearly heard the word "Kate..Kate". She then smiled, but became more surprised when she heard the parrot saying "I love you Kate". The parrot repeated the sentence a few times. Kate sighed with a smile. She had a deep emotional response. She then realised that Ed loved her because the parrot was saying those words.

Kate mumbled to herself,

"The parrot must have heard these words frequently from Ed".

Kate was pleased and joyful. She has been waiting for such a moment to learn that she was loved by someone whom she trusted and had numerous things shared in common with.

Ed brought two mugs of coffee and placed them on the small coffee table in the room. He then raised his head towards Kate and said

"Come, please sit down," said Ed

Kate was staring at Ed and taking deeper breaths

"Is there something wrong, Kate?" asked Ed, straightening his body. He stood up then walked towards Kate. He saw her standing with a smile on her face and staring at him.

Ed came near Kate, who kept silent looking at him. He came closer to her and looked at her eyes without a blink. Kate was swimming in the joy of her emotions, which made her heart beat faster, while Ed was looking at her in surprise. Soon the parrot repeated, "I love you, Kate... I love you, Kate". Ed felt shy, embarrassed and nervous when he heard that. He then bent his face downwards for few seconds and raised it again. Ed saw Kate stepping closer to him. With his shaky nervous hands Ed held Kate's hands and raised them to his mouth and kissed them and looked at her while her smile widened

"Kate..Did you hear what the parrot was saying?" asked Ed

Kate kept staring at him, then came closer to him and her body touched his

"The parrot is waiting for your answer," said Ed very swiftly

"Ed, tell the parrot that I love it too. Yes, I do love whoever said that"

Kate raised her arms and put them over Ed's shoulder and round his neck and pulled him towards her. Ed raised his arms and placed them around her too and pulled her head towards his shoulder with his face touching hers. Ed felt the warmth of Kate's face travelling through his skin to his heart carrying waves of emotion throughout his body. His heart was beating faster while the drops of sweat were covering his forehead. Ed turned the other side of his face and placed his cheek on her other cheek.

"I love you, Kate .. I do love you. I have never fallen in love with any girl before. You are my first love"

"And the last, I hope," said Kate

"The last I promise. I promise. It's not easy to find a suitable partner who shares your views and habits especially at this age. Please promise me too"

"Yes, it is my first and last too"

Ed then pushed her head gently away from him and held her soft chin. His eyes went deep into hers. He went closer to her. Ed started to breathe in Kate's breath, which went deep into his body and relaxed him emotionally. Kate then closed her eyes as she was entering a trance under the emotional effect of waiting impatiently for the next act from Ed. Ed and Kate swam deeply in the ocean of emotions which raised their adrenaline, which made their heart rates faster without either of them being aware consciously of what was going on.

"My God, Kate! You are my beauty queen!"

"I love you, Ed"

"How lucky I am to have you in my arms and how lucky I am to be loved by you"

"I think the coffee is getting cold"

The parrot said again, "I love you Kate"

"Let us go and have our coffee," said Ed, who held Kate's hand and took her to the settee, where he seated her and sat close to her. He continued looking at her and said

"I couldn't believe it..I couldn't"

"Couldn't believe what, my love?"

"I couldn't believe I would fall in love with someone one day. I needed this love. I am now so happy and pleased. I need not to say I love you. Someone here is saying it on my behalf"

"Does the parrot need long to teach it to say words?"

"Only a few days"

"So you loved me for a few days only?"

"Honestly, Kate. I had some strange feeling on day one when I saw you in your consulting room, which was only a few weeks ago. But the feeling became stronger and went deep in my heart when you phoned me asking about my eyes"

"I usually don't phone my patients especially if an appointment to see me has already been arranged"

"So I am privileged"

"You are privileged because you are the first and the only man sitting in my heart"

"In all the chambers of your heart?"

"Not only in all the chambers of my heart but in every cell of my body"

After that emotional peak, Kate held the mug of coffee and had a sip then she said after a laugh, "God.. It's so cold. We must have been hugging and kissing for a while"

"Do you regret that?"

"Regret? Why should I regret this paradise?"

"Your words make me very happy and pleased. I feel quite different now. You know, Kate, I am 42 and have fallen in love for the first time in my life. I am mature and not a teenager, so I really know what love is. I missed being loved since my mother died when I was at the University"

"I am sorry to hear that"

"Of course, Kate. Your love for me is different from my mother's.. but still I feel I need to be loved and cared for by someone. I am a human being. I am sure you have the same feeling"

"Ed. You know what? I am so happy that I lost my keys. I suspect they are inside the house. This is the first time that it happened to me to leave my keys inside the house. Anyway, if it wasn't for the lost keys, we wouldn't have been together now"

"You must have been very excited at the time"

"Yes, you are right. I was excited and nervous as I suspected how you felt, but was not sure. Also I have never had a date with a man"

"Do you know your eyes are the most attractive part of your face?. It was your eyes that I couldn't resist when I saw you the first time"

"So the other parts of my body are ugly. Aren't they?"

"No. Please don't get me wrong. I know you are teasing me"

"Where will I sleep tonight?"

"OK, this is easy. You sleep in my bed and I sleep here on the sofa. My other bedrooms are unfurnished. I shall give you a pair of my pyjamas to wear. I think you need some rest. It is now past midnight"

"That Persian food we ate made me very sleepy" Kate yawned "Sorry I am yawning"

"OK, come with me to the bedroom," said Ed. He held her hand and accompanied her to the bedroom on the first floor. He opened one of the drawer and took a pair of pyjamas and gave them to Kate

"Ed. Do you know I am impressed by your tidiness?"

"I wasn't like this before. I was so disorganised. Incidentally, do you know I am dyslexic?"

"Yes, of course I do. I read about you on the net. I was so impressed by the speech you gave at the reception. So how did you change from disorganised to being tidy and meticulous?"

"Isn't it too late now to talk? You are about to sleep"

"No, please. Tell me as a bedtime story. I am eager to learn about you"

"OK, you sit down on the bed and I shall sit on the chair," said Ed, sitting on the only chair in the room

"Yes, Ed. Tell me," said Kate while she lifted her legs on the bed and crossed them over after taking her shoes off "Sorry Ed. I feel better now. Yes, Ed tell me"

"When I was diagnosed with dyslexia, my mother took me to a psychologist before the age of 10 to control my impulsiveness. Teachers often got frustrated with my behaviour in class. I was misunderstood by my classmates. But one thing never changed: my astounding analytical ability. Just before entering university however, my temperament changed. I became more reserved and quiet in class. I went from seeing psychologists to consultant psychiatrists. Numerous head scans and studies were conducted to account for the behavioural change I underwent. My mother was initially impressed with the resulting calmness in her son. The single event that divided the two behavioural eras of my life was a fateful day at school. I was able to think about things and my ability at problem solving improved. I became amazing at dealing with frustration. I was at the beginning an easily frustrated young boy but since the event I changed and became patient. It gave me more opportunity to bring out my positive traits. Since then I became more organised"

"This is very impressive. You are a hero. I am so lucky to have you and luckier to have fallen in love with you"

"OK, Kate, I told you a bedtime story, which was interesting, I believe. I shall now leave you in peace and will see you in the morning. There is an en-suite bathroom which you can use. I shall take my pyjamas and go next door to get changed"

"I am sorry, Ed. Please don't misunderstand me. I would have slept with you on the same bed but I told you of what my family is and how I was brought up"

"There is no need to apologise. I respect this and encourage it"

Ed took a pair of pyjamas and was about to leave the room but he soon turned round to Kate and held her then brought his lips to hers and gave her a nice deep kiss. Then he left the room after closing the door behind him.

Ed went to another room and changed into his pyjamas. He brought a blanket and lay down on the sofa, putting a cushion under his head. Ed soon left the sofa and walked to take the coffee mugs to the kitchen and washed them. He then placed them on the rack. As he turned round to leave the kitchen he saw Kate standing behind him wearing his pyjamas and staring at him

"Yes, darling. What's the problem?"

"Your story, Ed. I don't know. It was sad but had a happy ending. I have been thinking. It was your mother who made all the change. You owe a lot to your mother"

"God bless her soul. Her efforts didn't go down the drain"

"I am sure she would have been proud of you to see you in such a position, having been knighted"

"Especially if she had seen this beauty standing in front of me to be my...partner"

Kate kept looking at him then walked closer to him, held herself against him taking deep breaths. Ed pulled her softly into his arms and said, "You'd better go to sleep, Kate, and don't make me more excited and nervous, otherwise I can't resist what will be coming next"

"Emotions overcoming principles"

"I have to respect your principles and upbringing otherwise it won't be in our interests"

"Yes. You are right. I don't want to regret it all my life".

Ed then held her hand and took her to the bedroom then closed the door. He made his way to the sofa and lay down after switching off the light. He had his eyes opened looking at the ceiling while his mind began to remember the events of the evening like a cine film. He remembered every word Kate said to him. He was smiling when he imagined Kate's tone of voice echoing in his ears. Kate was a great event in his life. She was his first love. As a mature man, he wasn't thinking of Kate just as a casual love in his life. He was thinking seriously of getting married and hence abandoning his boring life. However, he decided to spend more time with her in order to explore if she would suit him completely. The other issue was if Kate would have a similar opinion about him and whether she was thinking along the same lines of having Ed as a husband. While swimming in those thoughts Ed felt tired and went to sleep. Kate on the other hand went to sleep immediately as she was tired.

While asleep, Ed felt someone pushing him. He opened his eyes to see Kate had pushed herself onto the sofa and was lying down beside him in her pyjamas. He immediately smiled and extended his left arm to under her neck and hugged her gently and softly.

"I love you so much. I couldn't resist coming down to you. I felt sorry for you lying down on the sofa while I was lying down in your bed"

"I love you even more," said Ed.

Suddenly they heard a whistling noise from the parrot.

"What's that?" asked Kate

"That is the parrot waking up. It starts making those noises and whistles as soon as it wakes up in the morning. Soon it will start talking if we don't pay attention to it. Just listen" Ed said

Then the parrot started saying "Kate, I love you," repeatedly

"Well Kate the parrot is saying it on my behalf"

"I love to hear it from you"

"I love you, Kate. I do"

"Oh..I remembered something. I think I might have dropped my keys in the restaurant last night. Can we go later to check, please?"

"What's the time now?" Ed then looked at the wall clock in the room and said "Oh'.. I never sleep that long. It's ten o'clock. The restaurant won't open until 12"

"I shall have a shower and get changed," said Kate, who then stood up to go upstairs to the bedroom.

"Good. You do that and I shall make some breakfast. How about a light breakfast so that we can have lunch out today?"

"That should be fine"

~Chapter 7~

The Wedding

At around 8.oopm on Sunday, Ed took Kate back to her house after they had spent an exciting day of being together. They both found themselves attracted to each other. Ed went back to work at his company on Monday and for him it was a rather busy day after a 4-week holiday. He didn't come back home until 9 pm. He was exhausted. Upon arrival he did his routine with the parrot to give it food and water. He then sat down thinking about the structural work of the of the Energy Secretary's project. His telephone rang

"Hello..Hi, Kate. I am sorry I couldn't speak to you today. I have just come home and have been very busy"

"I love you, Ed"

"I love you too. I can't forget the lovely weekend we had together"

"When am I going to see you again Ed?"

"I don't think it will be before the weekend"

"This is too long. I have to see you during the week because I am going to fly to Lisbon on Friday night for my sister's wedding and spend the long weekend there"

"Are you coming back on Monday Bank Holiday?"

"Yes"

"What time is your flight on Friday?"

"I am taking the last BA flight at seven in the evening"

"This will be from terminal 5"

"Yes, that is right"

"You didn't tell me you were flying to Lisbon this weekend"

"I didn't know until late last night when I received a phone call from my mother. I managed to book a business class seat this morning"

"OK. Can I see you at 4.30 on Friday afternoon when I shall take you to the airport?"

"What about seeing you any day before Friday?"

"I am afraid I am too busy. We shall plan to meet after you have come back from Lisbon"

"That is not fair. How can you resist not seeing me till Friday?"

"I wish you knew how busy I am currently"

"Keep in touch, Ed. How is the parrot?"

"Keeps saying, 'I love you Kate'"

Ed was not in favour of seeing Kate in his house during that week because he was busy with the Energy Secretary's project.

It was 9 pm on Tuesday when Ed was sitting at his desk at home. His mobile telephone rang with a call from Kate saying

"Hi Ed. Where are you?"

"At home"

"Have you had your dinner?"

"Not yet. I arrived fifteen minutes ago"

"OK, open the door. I am outside"

"Really?! What a surprise. Just wait, please"

Ed put the telephone down and hid all the papers of the project, which he had spread on the table. He then rushed to open the door. Kate rushed to Ed, hugged him and kissed him. She entered with a small cabin bag and a carrier bag.

"My God! Kate you are so gorgeous! Thanks for coming"

"You didn't want to see me till Friday. Did you? How can you cope and how can you resist seeing me hugging and kissing me and....me kissing you?"

Kate entered to hear the parrot saying, "I love you Kate".

"A nice welcome from Mr Parrot"

"I brought you some dinner. I haven't eaten yet"

"It's very kind of you, Kate. Thanks. You made my evening bright. Do you realise how much I shall value this visit of yours? You proved caring and a really kind lover"

"I am staying the night. I hope you don't have any objection"

"Objection?! Are you joking?"

She went to spread the food over the table. She then went to the kitchen looking for drink, "Do you have any drink?"

"Sorry, Kate.. nothing but H_2O"

"That's fine.. I prefer water rather than juice. You know the yogurt drink we had in the restaurant the other night was great" She brought a bottle of water and two glasses then started to eat with Ed.

"Do you cook?" asked Ed

"Yes, I do. I prefer home-made food over ready-made. It's healthier"

Kate and Ed ate their dinner then spent some time together. Kate then went to sleep in Ed's room and Ed slept on the sofa. In the morning both Ed and Kate left for work at 7.30 am. Ed promised to see her on Friday to take her to the airport as promised. At midday Ed received a phone call from Kate to say that she left her ring in his bathroom and asked him to keep it till she saw him on Friday.

As promised, Ed called at Kate's house 4.30pm on Friday to take her to the airport. Kate came out with her suit case. He drove her to the airport explaining to her how he would miss her during her absence and that he would be looking forwards to seeing her when she was back on Monday. Ed took the details of her return flight in order to pick her up from the airport upon arrival. He dropped her at the airport in the passenger drop bay

"My apologies I can't come with you inside the airport because I am in a hurry to go"

"You must have more important affairs than me, Ed"

"There is nothing and no one in my life more important than you my dear Kate"

"I shall miss you sorely, Ed"

"Don't forget to phone me please" Then he realised he should give her the ring which she left in the bathroom" Kate, here we are. This is your ring which you left in the bathroom"

Ed and Kate hugged and kissed each other then she went inside the airport with her suitcase. She went to check in and she was assigned seat 1A. She then proceeded to the business lounge and phoned Ed

"Hi, Ed. I am in the lounge waiting for my flight. Good, it's on time with no delay. Are you missing me?"

"I'll miss you badly. Please call me when you arrive. I shall trace your aircraft till its arrival"

"I am so tired. For some reason I couldn't sleep last night. I have to go now because it is the last call. The gate will be closed soon. Bye and kiss kiss kiss"

Kate went through the gate to the aircraft and occupied her seat; she was hoping no one would sit beside her. The door of the aircraft was closed. The aircraft started moving to the runway. Kate sat and relaxed with her seat belt fastened. She closed her eyes and was thinking of Ed. All the memories of the weekend and Tuesday night which she spent in his house were passing through her mind and she was remembering every minute of those events. She was smiling while the aircraft was taking off and going up in the sky. Then for the first time she began thinking of marrying Ed. She had the daydream of Ed proposing to her and of walking beside him as his bride. Her memory became full of different pictures of Ed. She was so tired that it was easy for her to relax. All of a sudden her relaxation was interrupted by a voice:

"Miss Kate Fernandes"

She opened her eyes to find two air stewardesses standing up in the aisle close to her with smiles on their faces

"Yes..It's me," said Kate in surprise

One of the stewardesses smiled and said

"I am afraid this seat beside you is not empty and is occupied. The passenger is here"

Within herself she wasn't happy to hear that but she shook her head and said

"It's nothing to do with me. It's fine. It's an empty seat. I thought it would remain empty"

"Before you express your lack of concern, wait to see who is going to occupy it," said the stewardess.

"Who is going to occupy the seat? Prince Charles?!" said Kate jokingly

"May be a more important person to you, madam!" said the air stewardess with a smile

This was followed by a great surprise for Kate when she saw Ed standing by the seat 1C. Kate opened her mouth and widened her eyes with great surprise and said

"What's going on, is that you?!" She pointed with her right index finger to Ed "...Ed? I am shocked.. Am I dreaming?" She looked through the window "We are up in the sky"

"No, you are not dreaming, madam. This is Sir Edward James Carpenter," said the stewardess

Ed soon came near Kate's seat and knelt down and held her hands. He then took a little jewellery box which was in the hand of the other stewardess. He opened it and a solitaire diamond ring appeared.

"Miss Kate Fernandes... will you marry me? I am Ed James Carpenter," Ed said, holding Kate's left hand with his right and holding the ring in his other hand "I repeat..will you marry me?"

"Oh..Oh.."Kate covered her upper lip with her lower one and started weeping from happiness then put her right hand over her mouth and looked at the stewardesses to see them smiling widely saying,"Say yes.. come on"

Kate didn't know what to do immediately. She extended her two arms around Ed and hugged him strongly, weeping with happiness and joy. Ed pushed her gently and asked her again, "Kate, will you marry me?"

"Yes..yes..yes. Of course yes. Who else will I get married to apart from you? Who else will you get married to apart from me?"

Everyone in the cabin who was watching including the stewardesses shouted "Hey!" and applauded the event. Ed then took the ring and put it on her left ring finger then hugged her and they began kissing.

"You are an angel aren't you, Ed? What a surprise! How did you arrange all this?"

"I booked my flight on-line when you told me on Monday and decided to propose to you during the journey and during the flight"

"Oh..my God. I swear to you I was dreaming of this event just before it happened. Hey wait. You left me in the airport. What did you do afterwards?"

"I took the car and was received by car park attendants as pre-arranged then I checked in. I had already informed British Airways of my plans to ensure seating together and the two stewardesses were waiting. I was sitting in a rear seat until the moment came when I moved"

"That was a clever plan. Oh..Ed I am so pleased. This was the moment I was waiting for."

"I was scared in case you refused my proposal and make me embarrassed"

"I refuse something I have been waiting for and dreaming of! You must be mad?. I am sure my parents and my sister will be overwhelmed with happiness. You will accompany me as my fiancé to my parents' then to my sister's wedding. Ah.. Ed you don't realise how happy I am. I am now really and truly flying in the sky. Incidentally, where did you leave the parrot?"

"I left it with my friend Ahmad. It was he who gave it to me as a gift, but I had to give him some lessons on how to look after it"

"What a clever plan! Ed you are amazing"

"Do you know it was so helpful when you left your ring in the bathroom? I took it for measuring the size of your finger when I bought you the ring"

The joy surrounding both Ed and Kate was great. Kate couldn't wait till she arrived in Lisbon and told her parents, who, like any parents, had been waiting impatiently for Kate to get married.

Upon arrival her sister and her mother were waiting for her in the airport. They welcomed her with a big hug and kissing. Ed was standing beside her. Kate with a very happy face and with a big smile introduced Ed to them

"This is Ed. Sir Edward James Carpenter. My fiancé"

Kate had to translate to her mother in Portuguese. Her sister, Elizabetta, shook hands joyfully with Ed

"You said Sir Edward. Is he a Sir?

"Yes, he was knighted by the Queen recently"

"But you didn't tell us you were engaged"

"He proposed to me during the flight. I myself wasn't expecting him to be with me on the flight. He surprised me"

Margarida had to translate every sentence to her mother who then shook hands with Ed and said in Portuguese translated into English by Kate:

"My mother says she is very pleased for me to get married and especially to a Sir Edward who was knighted by the queen. She says you must be very famous"

"Ed is a very hard worker. He is the deputy chairman of a big company," said Kate

"How long have you known him for?" said Margarida

"It is only four weeks but you won't believe it. He came to me as a patient. It is good that I had discharged him from my care before he proposed to me. In the United Kingdom it is not accepted for a doctor to have a relation with a patient"

Ed, Kate , Margarida and their mother went outside the airport. They all went in Margarida's car. Ed was sitting in the front seat with Margarida, who was driving, while Kate and her mother were sitting in the back seats talking in Portuguese.

"Please take me to a nearby hotel," said Ed to Margarida

"No way. What do you mean, a hotel? There is a spare room in our house for you," said Kate

"Yes of course. You are the fiancé of my sister. You are part of the family. Besides, we shall be very proud of having a Sir knighted by the Queen of the United Kingdom to be in our house and come to my wedding too. It is an honour," said Margarida

"Thanks. That is very kind of you. Congratulation, Margarida, on your wedding and I am really honoured to be one of the guests," said Ed

Margarida said a few sentences in Portuguese to her sister and mother then she turned her face to Ed and said

"I wish you knew what they are saying there in the back"

"What are they saying?"

"They were talking about you all the time. All compliments of course from Kate. My mum is very impressed by you. She says you are very handsome. She also was asking Kate if you..."

"Stop it, Margarida..I shall tell him that later, please," said Kate who jumped in to interrupt her sister and prevented her from continuing

"Why? Is it bad?" asked Ed

"No..no, it isn't," said Margarida, laughing "Kate will explain later"

"I will Ed. It's nothing important or serious, but it's not the right place to say it," said Kate, who then continued talking in Portuguese to her mother

They arrived at their apartment, where Kate's father was waiting for his daughter. He was in his eighties and was sitting on a chair. Kate went to her father and hugged and kissed him then introduced Ed to him as her fiancé. Kate's father welcomed him very much and was very pleased to learn Kate was engaged. Her father asked about the wedding, which Kate translated into English.

"I think we could do it in four months. In September if we found a suitable venue"

"September! Are you serious?!" said Kate with a big smile on her face

"Why are you surprised?" asked Ed

"I didn't realise that you were in such a hurry"

"Well if you prefer we shall still do it in September but next year"

Kate translated the conversation to her parents. Her mother said, "Noooooo" wagging with her finger.

"My mum says no. She wants the wedding as soon as possible," said Kate

"If everyone is happy with September then we shall make the plans and I leave it to Kate to decide where," said Ed.

"Kate..why weren't you pleased to have the wedding in September?" asked Ed

"Do you want the truth, Ed? I want it today rather than tomorrow," said Kate

"My God..Kate," said Margarida "What's the matter with you? You have just got engaged and you have known Ed only for the past four weeks, yet you want to be wed in 4 months?!"

"I love him," said Kate "I can't wait till I...Margarida, don't make me embarrassed. It is lucky that my parents don't understand English and don't translate to them."

"Shall we have dinner together? My parents haven't eaten yet," said Margarida

"Kate and I ate a lot during the flight, but I don't mind sitting with you nibbling something," said Ed

"OK I'll make you some coffee first," said Margarida and went to the kitchen

"Kate. What did your mother tell you that you objected Margarida's translating to me when we were in the car?" asked Ed

"Yes. You reminded me. She asked whether I had slept with you"

"And what did you say to her?"

"What do you mean by what did you say to her? Of course I said NO"

"Why did you lie?"

"I didn't lie. It's the truth!"

"What do you mean by it's the truth? No, it isn't. Do you remember when you came in the morning and forced yourself against me and lay down beside me on the sofa?"

"Ed. Come on. You know what she means. Do I need to explain?"

"Yes"

Kate looked at him with a little smile, then shook her head. Her mother asked her what the conversation between her and Ed was about

"See. Now my mum is asking what we were discussing"

"Well. Tell her. Tell her the truth"

Kate stared at Ed with a smile, then picked up a little cushion and threw it at him, then laughed.

After dinner, Ed was shown to his room in the flat where he would spend a few days till he went back with Kate to London on Monday.

"It's a pity I can't come and lie down beside you here," said Kate

"I personally don't want you to"

"Why not? Are you fed up with me?!"

"It's not that I am fed up. I mean its better that now we keep distant until the wedding in order to preserve and respect you and your family's principles. No sex before marriage"

"Well, we are not going to have sex. I just want to lie down and hug and kiss you"

"Do you realise how these actions stimulate me and make me nervous and anxious to have sex?"

"Same with me"

"Then stop them please and just wait till September"

"It's too long to wait four months"

"Then arrange the wedding for an earlier date if you so wish. I have no objection to having the wedding earlier than September"

"It all depends upon the availability of a venue. We shall be lucky if we find a venue in September"

"September is not a popular month for weddings as far as I know. This makes life easier"

"Have you thought of a place to go for the honeymoon?"

"No. What about you?"

"Not really"

"I think we shall probably have to have one week only for the honeymoon"

"You are so mean"

"Well. You don't realise the amount of work in our company"

"I am also important in your life. Am I not?"

"Yes, you are. OK. Think of a place then we shall discuss it when we are back in London"

Time went on pleasantly and quickly with Ed and Kate in Lisbon. They had good times together and with the family. The wedding of Margarida was conducted extremely well. The trip to Lisbon created an excellent chance for Kate's parents and relatives to get to know Ed, who was warmly welcomed and received by all. Kate's parents loved Ed. He was nice to them. The love and care of Kate towards Ed reached a significantly high level on this trip, to the extent that neither of them could be parted from the other.

Upon arrival in London at 5.00p.m. on Monday, Ed took Kate back to her house in

Gerard's Cross. He then went to Ahmad's house to take the parrot back. Ahmad showed his surprise when he saw Ed

"Ed. The parrot kept saying 'I love you Kate'. Who is Kate?" asked Ahmad

"Oh, yes, I didn't have the chance and the time to tell you. It all happened recently and quickly within the past 4 weeks. I proposed to her during the flight on my way to Lisbon. I shall inform you of the details later. She is a fantastic lady. That's all I can say now"

Ed took the parrot and was about to leave when Ahmad said,

"One other thing about the parrot. I don't know if you were aware of this or not"

"What is it now?"

"Every time my wife called me the parrot said my mobile telephone number correctly."

"Yes, I am aware of this. I trained it"

"You must have spent good time in training it"

"It is fun. Bye for now"

Ed went home with the parrot and arrived at 8.15 pm. He entered his house and placed the parrot in the sitting room where it was before. He then went to prepare some food for the parrot and fill its water cup. A few minutes later he received a phone call from Kate

"Hi Ed. Where are you?"

"Home. I got here fifteen minutes ago"

"I am so used to you and don't know what to do"

"I am used to you too, probably more than you are to me. Come if you can"

"There is no need to ask me. Open the door for me. I am outside"

Ed rushed to open the door, where he was met by a hug from Kate, who had come with her cabin bag suitcase as before.

"I think I might have to come and live with you here," said Kate, walking down to the entrance hall.

"No. I do not want you to"

"Why not?" said Kate turning her face in surprise to Ed. "Do you not love me anymore?"

"Come on. Don't say that. You know that is not true and far from being true"

"But why should I not come and live with you here?"

"I explained to you, Kate. Being together at this stage under the same roof, hugging kissing and you lying down with me on the sofa might trigger further action and we may end up making love. Something which neither you nor your family will be happy with. Do you remember what your mother said to you? You made a pledge to your family which you should honour. Principles are principles. I honour principles especially if they are accompanied by a pledge."

"My mother will kiss you if she hears what you have just said"

"I will kiss her too"

"For what?"

" For giving birth to you"

Kate and Ed laughed

"How about a bite to eat?" ask Kate

"Good idea. I am hungry"

"Let's go out for a quick meal"

Ed and Kate left the house at 9.00 pm to buy some fast food locally and came back. As previously, Kate spent the night asleep in Ed's bed while Ed slept on the sofa.

During the week Ed purchased a single bed which he placed in one of the four bedrooms in his house in order to use it when Kate spent the night in his house. Ed preferred that Kate should not spend the night in his house on weekdays because he wanted to concentrate on the project he was completing for the Energy Secretary.

During the week, Ed went to see Mr Davies briefly. He explained that he would commission a trustworthy structural engineer friend of his to do the work. Mr Davies agreed to pay the expenses but he confirmed to Ed that the ultimate responsibility of keeping the secret of the project was Ed's. This made Ed more cautious about keeping the project beyond the approach of any person including

Kate who was his future wife. He managed to commission his structural engineer friend to do the work and the friend promised to complete it within eight weeks.

Ed asked Kate to look for a venue for their wedding in September. She decided to spend the weekend at Ed's home to look for a venue on-line. She came to his house on Friday night and they went out for dinner at a Middle Eastern restaurant. When she came home with Ed at 10 pm she switched on her laptop and started looking for a venue.

"Ed. I noticed something outside your house," said Kate

"What is it, darling"

"You have CCTV. Haven't you?"

"Yes"

"Are you that important?"

"Am I not?"

"I don't mean that. Of course you are particularly to me personally"

"This is for my personal security because I feel lonely. However sometimes I may deal with highly sensitive work at home which needs to be protected and secured"

"Is it connected to the police?"

"Yes, it is"

"So the police are aware of me coming here!"

"There are cameras everywhere including the bedrooms"

"Oh my God. Why didn't you tell me this before?"

"So what?"

"What do you mean by so what? Aren't you jealous about me? I get changed in your bedroom and take off my clothes and yet I am seen by others? I don't even allow you to see me without clothes on. How can you let others watch me?"

"What special thing do you have which any other woman doesn't? There is nothing to hide"

Kate stopped what she was doing and looked at Ed sitting beside her, then stared at him seriously. He also had a serious expression on his face

"That is not a nice statement from you, Ed"

"I know," said Ed in a very quiet and soft voice

Kate kept looking at him angrily

"I wish my mum heard this conversation"

"She has same organs as all other women have"

"Do you know you are a strange man? I wasn't aware of that before"

"I know. It's your problem that you didn't know this about me"

Kate showed an angry face and kept staring at Ed, who was very calm and quiet and was looking at the computer. Soon Kate continued

"I think you went too far"

"No, I didn't"

"I can't take this any longer"

Ed kept silent. Soon the parrot said, "I love you, Kate." Ed laughed loudly and grabbed Kate, pulled her to him and put his lips on hers and gave her a warm kiss. Kate pushed him angrily

"How can you believe that there is a CCTV camera in the bedroom? Even if there is, how could I allow it to be there when you undress in the room?"

"I swear I would have left you if it was true"

"No, you wouldn't"

"Why?"

"Because you love me and I love you. Now stop this and let us look for a venue"

They sat down together looking for a venue till they managed to find a few which were available in September. Ed and Kate decided to visit those places next day in order to make a choice of one of them. It was 3.00 am in the morning of the Saturday when Ed and Kate decided to sleep. Ed accompanied Kate to the first floor of his house

"I am going to sleep in the bedroom tonight," said Ed while going up the stairs with Kate

"What about me?"

"You will sleep in the bedroom too"

"What do you mean?" asked Kate stopping halfway up the stairs

"Why did you stop? Is there something wrong?"

"You are winding me up"

"Calm down and be patient." Ed continued climbing the stairs up

"I am going to sleep on the sofa then," said Kate, standing still halfway up the stairs. Ed came down three steps, held Kate's hand and tried to pull her upstairs, but she refused to move

"Calm down. I am going to sleep in the room next to you. I bought a bed for me to use when you come to stay with me"

Kate moved up when she heard that but with an angry face. Ed went up to the room next to the master bedroom which she was going to sleep in. Ed came to his bedroom and knocked on the door

"Can I take my pyjamas?"

"Just wait, please," said Kate. She went to hide in the en-suite bathroom while Ed was taking his pyjamas. He then left the room. Kate went to take a shower then dressed in her nightdress which she brought with her and went to bed. She gave a deep sigh while resting in bed and began to think about Ed's honesty. What an honourable man he was. He had no experience with any woman before.

There she was lying down in her nightdress on his bed and she was his fiancée yet he didn't touch her. She wished her parents knew about Ed's attitude, which was rarely found in a man.

"Every minute that passes I feel I love Ed more and more. He is the right man and he suits me. I don't know, I am a bit crazy sometimes and lose my temper easily". She went to sleep.

Ed was awaken by the soft voice of Kate

"Ed.. Ed"

He opened his eyes to find Kate standing up in her nightdress by his bed

"Yes, Kate?"

"I can hear some noises"

"Where?"

"I don't know. They're coming from outside"

Ed stood up and left his bed to accompany her to his bedroom where she was sleeping and went to the window

"Is it this noise?"

"Yes"

"This is the wind hitting that large tree. Calm down, please, and go to sleep"

He left her and went to his room and lay down in bed. A few minutes later Ed heard

"Ed..Ed"

Ed opened his eyes to find Kate standing by his bed again

"Now what is it, darling?

"I am sorry. I was a bit angry and lost my temper"

"That is OK. Forget about it. You are my love and my life. I don't take notice of these things. I apologise because I wound you up. Go and rest"

"I can't go to sleep because I feel guilty"

"I told you I did not take notice of that"

Kate pushed Ed and tried to come and lay down beside him

"No. Kate please. You won't do that. I don't accept it. You are in your nightie and...and..very attractive. I have never had any previous experience with a woman"

Kate did not pay attention to what Ed said. She pushed and lay in his bed. Ed stood up and said,

"OK, if you insist. Either you go and put on my pyjamas or I go and sleep in your place"

Kate remained in the bed and didn't take any notice of what Ed said. Ed then left the room and went to sleep in the double bed in the master bedroom where Kate had been sleeping. A few minutes later, Ed felt Kate pushing herself under the blanket behind him and hugging him firmly.

"Turn your face to me. I am scared to sleep alone. Turn your face to me please"

"Kate. You slept alone all your life in that big house of yours. Now you are scared to sleep alone in my house with me present on the premises and in the room beside my room?"

"I am used to my house but not to yours," said Kate very softly and in an attractive voice trying to seduce Ed, who kept himself in place with his back to Kate "Come on. Turn your face to me. I need you, Ed. I need you badly"

"You are here with me under the same blanket. That is enough. If I turn my face to you, you will be responsible for the consequences"

"I don't care. I need you. Come on. Ed. Please turn your face to me"

Ed didn't comply but within himself he was resisting his desire against the seduction of a half-naked lady with her night dress on lying in bed under the warmth of the blanket with her body touching his body firmly and her arms round him.

"Come on. Ed. Turn your face to me, please. OK. Just give me a kiss, then I shall leave you alone"

"Promise?"

"Yes"

Kate felt that she needed to fulfil her desire especially with her fiancé lying there in bed and she was ready to start a practice which she was dreaming one day of experiencing.

As soon as Ed turned his whole body to her she hugged him firmly, Her emotions were powerful. Her sexual feeling reached its peak. Ed was equally seduced by her. Kate then pushed herself over him and made him lie flat. Then, he felt her hand undoing the buttons of his pyjama top. He thought she was doing that to place her head over his chest. But as Kate was trying to take off her nightie, Ed immediately stopped her, held her arms and tried to push her aside

"Kate..Kate. Please, what are you doing?"

"Ed..Ed. Don't stop me. It's unfair of you to resist my desire. I need you. I need you badly."

Ed pushed Kate on one side and stood up.

"You may think I am an abnormal person when resisting a naked woman who is with me in bed. If that's what you think, you are wrong. Remember, Kate. Principles are principles. You had a pledge with your parents which you should honour. You believed in those principles which you said they were religious and which you made me strongly believe in. What do you think your parents will say when they hear about this?"

"I don't care. You are horrible to me..horrible. Aren't you a human being? Don't you have emotions and feelings? Why don't you respect my feelings?"

"Kate, please. Don't let a momentary pleasure make you regretful all your life. I am only defending your principles. Principles should be stronger than emotions" Ed said leaving the room and making for to the room where he slept in.

When he lay down he felt sorry for Kate and himself, as he desired nothing more than to make love to Kate but strongly believed that her parents' desire and principles must be honoured. Ed went to sleep and woke up at 11.00 am. He went quietly to see Kate, but she was not in bed. He heard the shower running. He came near the bathroom door and shouted

"Hi, Kate. Good morning"

"Good morning, darling. Come in. I am in the shower"

"I shall go down and wait for you"

"Come in, please, and hand me the towel. It's on the bed"

"You come out and get it"

"Don't be horrible. Hand me the towel".

He found the towel, which he took and stood outside the bathroom. He knocked on the door and shouted

"I am here standing outside the bathroom with the towel. Come and get it"

"I can't. Please bring it to me"

"I am standing here. If you are not coming to get it, I shall leave it on the bed and go downstairs".

After a minute she turned off the shower and came to the door. She opened the door widely while Ed placed his hand over his closed eyes and with his other hand held out the towel to her. Kate grabbed his hand, trying to remove his hand from his eyes and pushing him towards the bed, but he was quicker than her and left the room laughing and heard her shouting

"You are horrible to me," said Kate laughingly.

Ed went down to the ground floor then to the parrot, which was awake, and heard it saying,

"Good morning. I love you, Kate"

Ed went to the kitchen to prepare breakfast. He boiled 2 eggs and made some toast. He also made tea. As he was making a smoothie he felt Kate's soft hands round his neck. She then turned him round to face her and gave him a kiss and hug

"You were so horrible to me last night. I have never seen a man as strong as you are resisting his desire and seduction by a half-naked girl"

"Principles should be stronger than emotions. It was you who said that from the beginning and it was confirmed by your mother in Lisbon. You should stick to such principles"

"I apologise, but you are now so important in my eyes. Do you know why?"

"Why?"

"Because I am certain that if I leave you among thousands of naked young girls you will not touch any of them. I am so lucky to have you as a fiancé then a husband. So lucky. You are loyal. You proved to me how loyal you will be to me"

"Loyalty, my dear Kate, is an important principle. It starts from loyalty to your house, your wife and family, to your work and to your country. My involvement in some of my projects gave me the strength of being loyal, which I am proud of"

"My mother will be very pleased if she learns about what happened this morning"

"You will not tell your mum. Will you?"

"Of course not. If I do she will slap me on my bottom. But still. I felt badly I wanted you to make love to me. The desire was so great and irresistible. I felt I was boiling with desire which I badly needed you to fulfil. Unfortunately you didn't"

"If I were you I would have said, 'Fortunately you didn't'. Come on now, let us have breakfast then proceed to view those venues for our wedding party"

After breakfast Ed and Kate set off to visit a few places in the surrounding regions and Hertfordshire and managed to decide on a venue. Kate was very pleased and they both went to a restaurant to have dinner. Kate decided to spend the night at Ed's house.

"Can we sleep together in the same bed? Just for tonight, please," said Kate

"No. This will never happen until the honeymoon"

"OK. I shall wear Pyjamas"

"Still no"

"My God..You are really very strong"

"Life taught me to be strong. Staying firm to defend your principle against your emotion is a strength. You have to learn this. Wait. Didn't you say that in your faith sex before marriage was forbidden?"

"Yes, I did"

"Only on Saturday night before we went to bed you were defending this and went mad when you saw me going upstairs to sleep. You thought I was sharing a bed with you. Didn't this happen?"

"Yes, it did"

"So what made you change?"

"You...your body and my desire"

"You should defend your principles. You have to learn. Now go to sleep"

Ed was certain that Kate had to learn her lesson, which would always be beneficial to her. He was very pleased with the positive achievement he accomplished in teaching Kate. He knew he was resisting his desire and Kate's seduction, which was very difficult for him, but the achievement he acquired in teaching Kate a lesson gave him a strong feeling of satisfaction. As a person who believed he was loyal to the United Kingdom and proved his loyalty by making the plans for the Energy Secretary's big project, he was eager for Kate, his future wife, to follow in his footsteps and learn to be loyal to her principles, which would in turn teaches her to be loyal to her parents, her work and her country.

Kate and Ed went to sleep in separate rooms. Kate learned her lesson and began to realise that Ed was in fact on her side rather than against her. Ultimately fulfilling a desire was only a temporary event, while standing firm for a principle was an everlasting issue.

Ed decided to have the forthcoming few weekends devoted solely to his work together with the structural engineer friend of his. Kate was saddened by the news that Ed would be busy for a few weekends. She accordingly decided to spend two nights during the weekdays every week at Ed's house, which was warmly welcomed by Ed.

In August and four weeks prior to the wedding date, Ed and the structural engineer completed the work. Ed had a meeting with the Energy Secretary, who approved the structural work with joy and informed Ed that the project would be discussed in the forthcoming meeting of the Cabinet. He congratulated Ed for his excellent work and effort but again he pointed out it was Ed's responsibility to store all the information safely and in his own possession. Mr Davies was pleased to be one of the invited guests at Ed's wedding.

While preparing for the wedding was mainly the responsibility of Kate, Ed was busy with thinking of the method in which he would store the original documents of the project, the plans and the structural calculation, in a safe secured place. He was thinking of different options but thought that storing the project papers in his house was not a good option because he would be vulnerable. In case of any burglary or fire the information might disappear. He was not in favour of storing them at Kate's house because he did not want any issue related to the project to be known to Kate or any other person apart from himself. He then thought of hiring a fixed safety box in a bank but the information and the plans were extensive, so he decided to store all the original documents on a CD and a USB stick and store them in a safety box at a bank. However, there was still one problem namely the safety password which he would be given by the bank and which he had to store somewhere. He was apprehensive and concerned because he might fail to recall the password; especially he was busy and dyslexic, then in such an event there would be a big problem. He also was not in favour of storing the password and the PIN number in any place at his home because of the possibility of their being stolen or disappearing in a fire or a burglary.

Ed remained in a dilemma for a few days. Kate began to notice that Ed was anxious and nervous. He looked as if something was occupying his mind. Ed wasn't paying the full attention he used to pay to Kate. This was one reason why Kate was concerned and started questioning what was going on.

"Darling. You don't look yourself," said Kate. Ed was not paying attention and was keeping quiet, staring into a corner "Ed. Are you OK?"

"Yes I am OK"

"I don't believe it. I am your fiancée and I know a lot about you. You are not Ed whom I knew before. Please be frank, open and honest with me. In a month I shall be your wife."

"I have some problems at work which I need to resolve"

"Talk to me I might be able to help you"

Ed stood up and walked towards the corner where the parrot's cage was placed. Kate followed him and stood behind him then put her right hand over his right shoulder and turned him round towards her. She then lifted his chin with her right hand to look at his eyes

"Ed. Darling. I have never seen you in such a state before. Have you discussed the problems with someone at work like the Chairman John Basing or even your friend..Ahmad?"

As soon as Kate finished saying Ahmad, the parrot pronounced Ahmad's telephone number. "What?" said Kate, turning her face with a rather surprised look at the parrot "What did the parrot say?"

When Ed heard Ahmad's telephone number from the parrot, he opened his eyes wide and stopped moving as if he was paralysed for a few seconds. He was staring in front of him. Then a gradual smile appeared on his face as if he had discovered something. Then he shouted

" Yes!..yes!..I've got it...I've got it" He held Kate's arms and pulled her towards him "I love you, Kate..I love you, Kate"

The parrot repeated "I love you, Kate"

Ed then gave Kate a strong hug followed by a nice kiss

"Yes, you are my fiancée and you should always stand by me"

"It is truly said that there is a woman behind each great man"

"It's correct, it's correct," said Ed. He then turned his face to the parrot "I love you, Mr Parrot. I really love you"

The parrot kept repeating "I love you, Kate"

Kate was very pleased and smiled at the sudden change in Ed's behaviour and appearance.

"Kate. Today is Friday. Did you bring your stuff to spend the weekend here?"

"No. Because I thought I can't come over at the weekends"

"But the busy weekend work is over now"

"So I can stay tonight!"

"Yes, of course"

"Let us go and get your clothes and other belongings, then we go for dinner, then come here for the rest of the weekend"

"We can then make further plans for the wedding"

"Yes of course. Come on, let us go. It is nine o'clock already. By the time we are back it will be midnight"

"And we can sleep in one bed!"

"No. This is impossible," said Ed, then held Kate's hands and pulled her towards the door "Be patient woman. It's only four weeks till we sleep not just together but...I don't want to say"

"Please just tonight together. No love-making I promise"

"I said no. Don't make me change my mind"

As he was leaving the house, Ed shouted "I love you, parrot"

The parrot said, "I love you, Kate"

Kate drove her car this time with Ed sitting beside her. While she went to collect her stuff from her bedroom in her house, Ed waited for her in the sitting room. Ed was thinking with joy and happiness of the possibility of solving the problem. It was the parrot which was the key issue. He would teach the parrot the PIN number and the password for the bank safety box and would have to teach it a cue to disclose the number. That cue would only be known to Ed and the parrot. Ed reckoned that that wouldn't be difficult because of his previous experience with the parrot in memorising telephone numbers and acting as a telephone directory. It would therefore be just a matter of training the parrot.

Kate came down with her cabin bag and was pleased to see Ed smiling. The couple left for dinner then went to Ed's house. They sat down discussing their plans for the wedding

"Ed. Where shall we stay after our honeymoon? In my or your house?"

"Mine, of course"

"Why of course? Please, Ed. Don't get offended. I think Gerard's Cross is a more reputable area than Slough. Do you mind if we stay in my house?"

Ed had a little think. He would not need the security and the CCTV if he were to stay in Kate's house. Therefore it would not be a problem if he lived with Kate in Gerard's Cross.

"That should be OK. I can join you in Gerard's Cross"

"Lovely and fantastic. But every now and then my mother may come to spend a few days with us. I hope there will be no objection"

"It's your house. You have the right to do anything in it and bring anyone of your family. You can even kick me out of it if you so wish"

"Go away. How can I do that? You are now part of me. Part of my life and my soul"

"Now the time is approaching two in the morning. Let us go to sleep and continue our discussion tomorrow"

Ed and Kate went to the first floor. Ed kissed Kate and said to her, "Goodnight"

Kate stopped and didn't move

"What's the matter, Kate?"

"You and I sleep together in the room"

Ed looked at her then shook his head, meaning "No". Then he left her and went to his room. Immediately he came and knocked on the Kate's door

"Can I come in to take my pyjamas?"

"Do come in"

Ed opened the door to find Kate in her underwear as she was getting changed to wear her night dress. He immediately closed the door and went to his room. Kate then followed him immediately in her bra and knickers but he asked her to leave his room immediately and pushed her out of his room and closed his door. Ed then lay down in his trousers after taking his jacket off. After a while Kate knocked on his door.

"I am not opening it. Go back please"

"Open the door. I am in my nightie"

"Still. Please leave my pyjamas outside the room and go"

"I am in my nightie and I am not coming into your room. Open the door"

After a brief silence he opened the door and it was a surprise to see Kate standing outside the room carrying his pyjamas. She handed in his pyjamas then grabbed him and gave him a long kiss, then left him and went back to bed. Ed then got changed and lay down in bed in joy and happiness because his problem in keeping all the information about the project was solved. He went to sleep.

Ed and Kate continued their effort to produce a list of the guests to their wedding party. Kate spent her weekends in Ed's house, but without asking him to sleep together as she had learnt her lesson.

As planned, Ed spent a few evenings saving all the information about the project on USB and CD. He then took them to a bank and saved them in a safety box. He came home to train the parrot on the PIN number 27351981. He trained the parrot using a cue of "bank". Then he began testing the parrot. After a few days of training he managed to make the parrot say the PIN number every time Ed said "bank". He also tested the parrot by saying similar words such as "sank", "rank", "tank". He was pleased because although those three words would rhyme with "bank", the parrot was able to differentiate them from "bank". Additionally to strengthen the security he used an encrypted USB stick and CD and trained the parrot so that when the cue of "USB" was said it then pronounced the PIN number. In any case Ed's plan was that the parrot would stay with him and it would be impossible for anyone to know what the cue was. With that the secret would be buried completely. Ed was so pleased.

The wedding ceremony was great. Kate was wed to Ed. Kate's parents and sister and her husband were all present besides a few of her Portuguese relatives, who travelled from Lisbon. Most of the employees of the United Architects were present too, including Mr John Basing and his only friend Ahmad and his wife. The day after the ceremony Kate and Ed went on honeymoon to South Africa where they spent two weeks. As before, Ed asked Ahmad to look after the parrot and Ahmad happily accepted the task.

Ed and Kate arrived at their hotel in Cape Town. Ed had hired a suite as a surprise for Kate. They entered the suite and closed the door. Kate held Ed with her two hands and said

"Now you won't run away. There are no more excuses. I am so frustrated" Kate pushed Ed to the bed and laid him down. She took off his jacket then his shirt. She was so pleased because unlike before there was no objection or resistance from Ed.

"Wait, Kate, let me take off my shoes and socks"

"Go on then"

While he was taking off his shoes, socks and trousers, Kate was taking off her dress. Ed lay down on the bed without any resistance. Kate came to him in her underwear and threw herself on Ed, putting her two hands on his forearms. She then brought her face near his. Ed was smelling her breath. She brought her lips to his. Their sexual desire went in to flame of sexual attraction. Kate then had what she was dreaming of before, a joy which made her fly over the moon in love and emotions. This time without any objection or resistance from Ed; on the contrary Ed was deeply involved in the emotion and satisfied himself with flares of joy and happiness that came uniquely from Kate

~Chapter 8~

The Separation

U pon their return from their 2-week honeymoon, Kate and Ed felt closely attached to each other. The love, emotion and care flared up and reached their peak. This was not unexpected in such a mature couple who had been in love for a few months only and who had had no experience of sex previously. Kate was so pleased that upon her return she was begging Ed to extend his holiday for another week as she had another week of holiday but Ed was unable to fulfil her request because of the workload from the company. However, he managed to be more flexible and came back home between 4 and 5 pm every afternoon and took the Friday off work. This arrangement gave Kate some satisfaction in fulfilling her desire to spend more time with Ed. During the week, Kate and Ed managed to move all his property except for the beds to Kate's house including the parrot, which, to Ed was the most valuable possession, although Kate, like everyone else, was unaware of the reason. The parrot was placed in a corner in the sitting room and it was Ed's duty to look after it by feeding it, cleaning the cage and taking it once monthly to the veterinary clinic for cleaning, cutting its claws and a general check-up. Ed continued to keep the parrot memorising the PIN numbers for the safety box and the USB of the secret project by saying the cues of "bank" and "USB" to the parrot. Ed ensured that he kept those cues and the PIN numbers away from Kate's knowledge. For this reason, he used to talk to the parrot when Kate was away. Being newly married to Ed, whom she loved a lot and wanted to please, she spent a few hours purchasing some underwear and nightdresses which she knew would make her alluring in Ed's eyes. She also began to practise her expertise in cooking. She bought a cookery book of Indian and Middle Eastern dishes and began to cook. It was her best time of the week when she was lying in bed beside Ed under one blanket with her body pressed against his, feeling its warmth and going to sleep triggered by the ticking of his heart, which she often commented on

"Ed. I can feel your heart ticking"

"This is probably because you are a doctor. I can't feel yours. At least it means I am still alive"

"It seems that your heart beating will be my triggering stimulus to put me to sleep"

"This is not good"

"Why not good?"

"Because you will not be able to go to sleep if I am away"

"On the contrary. This is very good because I will have to follow you anywhere you go otherwise I shall suffer from insomnia"

"Is this one of your tricks to keep you with me all the time?"

"Wait till you see more coming"

Although Kate was 40 years old, like any female she was eager to become pregnant and practise her motherhood. Her mother's dream was that Kate one day would give birth to her first grandchild. Kate was aware, however, that age was an important concern and that there might be a chance of her having a child with some form of congenital defects like Down's syndrome. That was Kate's fear and concern in case she became pregnant, although she did not disclose that information to Ed. She rather preferred to leave any possibility of pregnancy to chance.

Kate's expectations came true. Three months after the honeymoon she missed her period but kept it quiet from Ed. However, soon the information had to be disclosed to Ed because a few weeks later she began to experience morning sickness and the pregnancy was ascertained by a positive pregnancy test.

"What is the problem Kate? You feel sick every morning"

"I don't know if you would feel happy or sad if I told you the reason"

"You make me laugh, Kate. How can I be happy observing you retching and vomiting every morning?"

"We came back from our honeymoon nearly five months ago and we are sexually very active, aren't we?"

"I think so, but I don't understand. Are you feeling sick because we are sexually active? We can stop making love if it brings you relief," said Ed with a strained smile on his face

"No, Ed. You don't understand. Only ladies will understand. Do you have a clue now?"

"I still don't understand"

"Ed. You are going to be a father," said Kate, staring at Ed's face and observing his reaction eagerly

"No! Is that true?" said Ed after few seconds of staring at Kate with his eyes wide open. Then a smile started to spread across his face "Kate. Are you pregnant?"

"Yes, my love. I am"

Ed stood and went to hug Kate strongly and kiss her on her cheeks then kissed her lips strongly and held her between his arms. He gave a deep sigh

"Oh! It's my dream which is coming true"

"Ed! Are you really happy about my pregnancy?"

"Of course I am like any man. I wish my mother were alive to learn about this. She would have been happier than anyone else"

"I didn't realise you would be pleased"

"What makes you think that?"

"I don't know but lots of men think that way"

"I am not one of them"

"I have to phone my mother. She will be pleased about this. She has been dreaming of having her first grandchild through me"

"Your sister Margarida got married a few months before us. She may be pregnant by now"

"No, she is not yet. I think the problem is probably her husband"

"Poor Margarida. Give her a chance. She might become pregnant one day"

"But I am glad that I became pregnant before her. My mother's dream came true"

"I am very pleased that we didn't make love before the wedding otherwise you would have been in trouble being pregnant and yet not married"

"Yes. I agree. I think you were very wise in opposing it. I was so desperate and frustrated at the time"

"Patience and perseverance are very important qualities of mankind which differentiate us from animals"

"I learned my lesson. I am so happy now"

"I think the parrot will also be pleased with this"

"What does the parrot have to do with my pregnancy?"

"The parrot will be pleased to have a company at home, you and our child. The poor parrot feels lonely when no one is at home"

"So you want me to have a baby to please the parrot?"

"I hope you are not serious in what you have just said!"

"I may be because of what I have heard"

"Come on Kate. Don't be silly"

"I shall now have to report to my doctor and I am certain I shall be referred to an antenatal clinic. I have a gynaecologist friends of mine who will look after me if and when needed. I shall talk to one of them"

"That will be good although I don't have much knowledge in this field. I have never become pregnant before," said Ed

"I think now we have to think of a name for the baby. What about..."

"Charles or William?"

"It seems you like the names of the royal family"

"No, but these names just came to my mind"

"And what about if the baby was a female?"

"My mother's name was Rebecca Anna"

"Nice names. Both Biblical names"

"Anyway, names are not so important now. We can wait till nearer to your delivery"

"I think I shall do some research. I would like names which are not common"

Kate's pleasure peaked when she learned of Ed's happiness about her pregnancy. She phoned her mother in Lisbon to inform her of the news. Her mother was so joyful and happy. She gave her advice on how she should care for herself and eat properly.

Kate attended the antenatal clinic when she was eight weeks pregnant and was given an appointment for her first antenatal scan when she would be 12 week pregnant. She was happy when she came home in the evening to see Ed

"I am not pleased with this parrot"

"Why?"

"It has an evil eye. It keeps looking at me"

"Kate. What is the matter with you? It is just a harmless animal. In addition it keeps us company"

"I was given an appointment for a scan of the baby in four weeks"

"Good. It will tell us its sex"

"It's too early for this. You won't be able to tell yet. Are you eager to know the sex now?"

"Not really"

An hour later Kate felt some abdominal pain. At the beginning she thought it was just a vague ache or wind. She took two tablets of paracetamol but the pain was not relieved. She went to sleep till 3.00 am, when she woke up to tell Ed of the increasing severity of the pain. She couldn't continue to sleep then left her bed, with Ed accompanying her to the ground floor. After an hour, the pain was concentrating in the left lower side of her tummy.

"Ed. Please take me to a hospital soon. I don't think the outlook is good"

"What do you mean?"

"I hate to say it. I hope it's not what is in my mind"

Ed soon helped her to get changed then took her in his car to a nearby hospital. She was admitted immediately and after an urgent abdominal scan the diagnosis of ectopic pregnancy was made. She was taken to the theatre and an operation was carried out to excise the left-sided ectopic pregnancy. Ed then went and sat with her until she woke up from the anaesthetic and spoke to her

"I am very pleased that you are fine, nice and safe"

"I am not, Ed. I am not," said Kate, then started weeping.

"Please, Kate. It's OK now," said Ed while placing his hand on her forehead and passing his right palm across her head softly and gently "Most importantly you are safe and there are no complications"

"Ed. You are not going to become a father. I am not becoming a mother"

"So what Kate!? So what? My priority is you. To me you are my world and my whole life"

"It's shocking and depressing"

"I sympathize with you but it's out of our control. You will become pregnant again as long as we continue making love. You have two ovaries and two tubes. I learned that the pregnancy was in your left tube"

"I am not certain of my chances becoming pregnant again. My mother will be upset and depressed"

When Kate was discharged, Ed took one week of holiday to remain beside Kate who was in great need of having Ed by her side. She received a visit from a gynaecologist friend of hers, who informed Kate that 65-85% of women became pregnant after an ectopic pregnancy and that this might happen within 18 months from excising an ectopic pregnancy. This information soothed Kate but the gynaecologist informed Ed that Kate was depressed, which was not uncommon after ectopic pregnancy excision or after miscarriage and that Kate needed special attention.

A few days later Kate's mother came from Lisbon to stay with her. This was a relief to Ed, who wanted to go back to work and also thought that the presence of Kate's mother would provide good psychological support for Kate. Kate's mother planned to stay for a few weeks till Kate was ready to cope with her daily activities.

Despite her mother's presence, Kate became very depressed and wept easily. A few times she cried loudly. Two weeks after her mother's stay, Kate told Ed

"Ed. Do you remember when I told you about the parrot?"

"No, I don't. What did you say?"

"I don't like it. It has an evil eye"

"Kate. You are a wise woman and very efficient consultant ophthalmologist. I don't think it is wise you say things like that about a friendly and harmless bird"

"That doesn't matter. Even my mother said the same"

"At least it keeps saying 'I love you, Kate'. This sentence should give you some happiness in my absence from the house during the day"

"I don't care. I don't like this bird"

"I was pleased with what the gynaecologist said the other day about the good chance of you becoming pregnant again," said Ed in an attempt to change the subject and allow Kate's mind to drift away from the parrot

"Yes, but it's not a hundred percent chance"

"Please be optimistic like me. I have always been optimistic in my life"

"Don't leave me, Ed. I need you badly"

"You are aware how much I love you. Kate. Forget about pregnancy now. I am certain you will become pregnant and we shall have our child"

"I shall be nearly forty-two by the time I become pregnant again and give birth to a baby, if I become pregnant"

"We were told within 18 months. You may become pregnant at any time"

"Yes, but the chance of abnormal pregnancy and abnormal foetus increases with advancing age of the pregnant lady"

"Kate. Please stop practising medicine on yourself. This is the problem when you are a doctor. Keep yourself to eye disease only, which is your speciality"

Kate's depression became severer than before. She went with Ed to see a psychiatrist. At first the psychiatrist was not in favour of starting her on medications as Kate was not in favour of taking them in addition to the possible side effects. She informed the psychiatrist that she believed the parrot was contributing to her problem. She explained her hatred for that bird. The psychiatrist later telephoned Ed to ask him to take the parrot out of the house because this might help to alleviate Kate's symptoms or even relieve them totally. This was because Kate was under the impression that her ectopic pregnancy might have been the result of the parrot's evil eye. Although Ed struggled to persuade Kate that it was impossible for her depression to be caused by the parrot, Kate was adamant about accepting the psychiatrist's suggestion. Ed found himself in a rather difficult situation. On the one hand the secret of the national project which was in the interest of the United Kingdom lay with that parrot. On the other hand his wife's illness might have been, as she believed, caused by the parrot's presence on her premises. He was not in favour of leaving the parrot in his own house and visiting it briefly once daily. If that happened, it would not secure the continuous care of that animal which was vital to him and to the United Kingdom's national security. Ed then thought of one possible solution, though it was temporary. He approached his friend Ahmad and asked him if he could look after the parrot for 2 weeks in order to find out if that would give a chance to Kate to get over her illness.

Ahmad and his wife Claire were happy to look after the parrot.

Ed took the parrot to Ahmad but Kate was still not pleased because she knew that the parrot would be back in two weeks. Kate was right in her expectation. She did not show any sign of improvement. Her claim against the parrot was encouraged by her mother who shared her views. During the two weeks when the parrot was with Ahmad, Ed used to go and visit Ahmad at home and ensured that the parrot was in safe hands and that it continued memorising the PIN numbers. That action took Ahmad by surprise. He wondered why Ed was highly concerned about the parrot although Ahmad was looking after it. When Ed took the parrot back after two weeks, a big argument developed between Ed and Kate in the presence of Ed's mother-in-law who was siding with her daughter against Ed

"I don't understand why you love this bird more than me," said Kate in an angry toned voice

"Listen, darling"

"Don't address me as darling. Your darling is the parrot"

"You are behaving like a child"

"You are aware that my depression is aggravated if not caused by that parrot. So keeping it here will not relieve the depression"

"My dear. You very well know that your depression followed the ectopic pregnancy and was not caused by the parrot. So stop blaming this poor animal"

"OK. Why is it so important to you?"

"This is simply because it grew up with me for the past year or so and it's not humanitarian behaviour to get rid of it"

"We can give it to the RSPCA"

"I will miss it if it is given to anyone"

"Ed. It's my life now which very much is dependent upon taking away this parrot from my premises."

"OK, darling. Can we leave it till tomorrow morning, Saturday? I shall give the matter some thought till the morning and there is no need to be nervous"

There was a discussion between Kate and her mother in Portuguese

"What is your mum saying?"

"She was asking about our discussion. She is pressing for getting rid of the parrot in favour of relieving my depression. Ed you do not seem to be helpful at all"

Ed did not reply but left the scene and went to the bedroom on the first floor. He lay down in bed and started thinking of how he could get out of that dilemma. The situation was difficult and within himself he was wondering what would happen if Kate was adamant in her decision that the parrot should leave the house. Ed eventually gave up and found himself powerless. He went to sleep

Kate and her mother had a discussion

"Ed is behaving strangely. Why is he so attached to the parrot?" Kate's mother said

"I don't know. I probably would have behaved the same way if I were him"

"He should put you first"

"Yes, I agree. Look, he has been in the bedroom alone for nearly an hour and a half. He hasn't done this before. Mum, I love him"

"He must choose between you and the parrot. If he loves you he will have to get rid of the parrot"

"Mum, I am improving. I feel a little better"

"Yes, don't you know why? Because the parrot was away. As you said, it has an evil eye"

When Kate went to her bedroom it took her by surprise to find Ed was deeply asleep. Ed had never gone to sleep previously without Kate.

In the morning Ed woke up while Kate was still asleep beside him. He left her and went down after getting changed. He went to the parrot and began practising it memorising the PIN numbers a few times. Ed was pleased to learn that the parrot was still remembering them. After an hour Kate came down to find Ed with the parrot. Without any hug or kiss Kate asked him

"What did you decide about the parrot?"

"Darling, please." He came near her and held her arms but she removed his hands and pushed them away

"You must now decide between me and the parrot"

"It is just an animal. It is very safe and nice. It says your name all the time. I don't think it would harm anyone"

"I can't see this bird in my house. Do you understand my health is deteriorating because of this parrot? Get it out now." Then she shouted "Now, immediately"

At this stage Kate's mother came down the stairs and sat down watching Ed and Kate arguing

"There is no need to become angry and nervous. It is not going to help your health at all"

"It's my house and I am free to decide who lives in it"

Ed looked at Kate, then gave a deep sigh and lowered his head

"Now what is your verdict, Sir Edward James Carpenter?"

"What if I refuse to get rid of the parrot?" said Ed after a short period of silence. He had realised that Kate was not in her right mind.

"Then you feel free to take your parrot and leave my house"

"OK, Miss Fernandes. I will. It's your house and it's your decision"

"You may do what suits you"

Kate was serious about her decision although she was testing Ed's loyalty to her. Ed went to the bedroom and put most of his clothes and belongings in a suitcase and brought it down the stairs and was heading towards the main house door. He then carried his laptop in its case, opened the door and placed everything in the boot of his car on that rainy day. He then came back soaked in water with Kate and her mother watching him in surprise. Ed went to the parrot and picked up the cage and was about to leave. He turned his face to Kate, who turned her face sideways in anger when she saw Ed looking at her. At that point the parrot shouted "I love you, Kate" a few times. Ed kept looking at Kate then put the cage on the floor and went to Kate and stared at her and wanted to kiss her but she refused and pushed him away.

"Remember, Kate. I always loved you. You were my first and last love. However, you kicked me out of your house. Bye for now"

Ed then turned his face to his mother-in-law and said, "Bye, Mrs Fernandes".

He then turned his face to Kate and said "Thanks for having me on board all this time"

As Ed arrived at the door he put his left hand in his pocket and took a key ring out with two keys on. Ed then turned round and walked back and put the keys on a coffee table

"These are the keys to your house, Kate"

Ed carried the cage and left the house for his car, where he placed the cage on the back seat and left, heading to his own house.

Kate and her mother looked at each other

"He has left, Kate. He's gone," said Kate's mother

"I know," said Kate then burst to tears "I know. But I love him. I do love him"

"Don't worry. He will come back" Kate's mother walked to Kate and held her to calm her down

"No, Mum, no. You don't know Ed. I know him very well. He has a very strong personality. I have experience with him. He can resist anything and stays strong. I know he loves me"

"What is the problem with him? Why does he love the parrot?"

"I don't know, Mum. This is very strange. I don't think it's a matter of love. I may ask Ahmad who is his only friend"

"He will come back"

"I don't think so. He even left the keys here. It was my fault because I asked him to leave"

"Why did you do that? Are you mad? He is a very nice person"

"I am now more depressed than before but will not revoke my decision. I need him but not the parrot. If he wants to keep the parrot he won't have me"

Ed proved his loyalty to the United Kingdom and placed it over his emotions and preferred it over his wife. Although he was so sad at leaving Kate, especially as she was in that state, he was tranquil because he preferred his loyalty to his country. He was also happy because Kate was not alone. He was pleased about Kate's mother looking after her at that difficult moment in her life. Ed was confident that the situation might be resolved if the responsibility of keeping the documents were taken away from him. However he wasn't certain if Kate would revoke her decision subsequently. It was difficult for him to get the parrot out of his life in any way.

Ed, who loved Kate was in a dilemma. He felt very lonely at home because he was used to Kate. His memories of the past with Kate were coming back to him. He remembered the first time he met Kate and how he proposed to her. The time of the honeymoon left a deep memory in his mind. He decided to continue his life now at least temporarily without Kate until he found a solution to the problem. He wasn't certain whether, Kate knew the secret behind keeping the parrot that would make her to reconsider her decision. He was apprehensive in case he told her about the secret and yet she continued firm regarding her decision. Ed therefore decided to give the matter some thoughts even if he had to discuss the issue with the Energy Secretary because his home life was wrecked and he was back to being a single man after being married for few months only. He was at that stage separated from his wife; the lady whom he had been dreaming of meeting and the only woman he had a relationship with.

Kate phoned Ahmad and asked to see him privately and in confidence. Ahmad came to visit Kate at her home.

"Thanks, Ahmad, for coming to visit me," said Kate

"Not at all. I am sorry to hear all about the operation you underwent. Claire and I meant to come and visit you but Ed said it wasn't the right time," said Ahmad

"Yes. That was followed by depression, which I think is getting better"

"Ed must still be at work"

"Ed won't come back"

"I don't understand. What do you mean by that? He was fine when I saw him today"

"Can I ask you something?"

"Of course, go ahead"

"Why does Ed love the parrot so much?"

"Oh, that parrot! I gave him the parrot as a gift when he was knighted and I think because he was lonely he was attached to it. Why do you ask that? Did something happen?"

"I don't like that parrot especially after what happened to me. I think it has evil eyes"

"No. It's a nice animal"

"Anyway that is my opinion"

"Which is highly respected"

"But Ed doesn't seem to respect my opinion"

"What do you mean?"

"He wants to keep the parrot despite my refusal to have it"

"Is that why Ed left home?"

"Yes. Is there something unique about this parrot? I see Ed talking to it. Once I saw him talking to it quietly as though he didn't want me to listen. That is why I couldn't stand it"

"I don't think there is anything more than that Ed is enjoying this talking animal. You should be pleased with it because it keeps saying, 'I love you Kate'."

"Can you find out please the reason behind Ed's love for this animal?"

"I will try but I still think that there is nothing special about it"

"Please don't tell Ed that you saw me. Please pretend you know nothing about what happened"

On the next day after a meeting with Ed, Ahmad asked Ed about Kate

"Incidentally how is Kate?"

"She is improving but still depressed"

"Claire and I want to invite you to come round for dinner if she is OK otherwise we shall come to visit her. We haven't seen her since her operation and her illness"

"Neither option is possible"

"Can I know why? Is it because she is still very unwell?"

"Ahmad, you are my only friend in life"

"I am aware of that"

"I have left home and moved back to my original house in Slough as a single man"

"When did this happen? I am sorry to hear about this"

"I had better discussed this outside the work because I am busy now"

"Can I come and visit you at home tonight?"

"Yes, of course"

"I shall bring you some dinner. You like the dolma"

"Excellent. I look forward to it. Eight o'clock will suit me fine"

Ahmad went to see Ed at his house at 8 pm as arranged and sat down to eat the dinner

"Now, Ed. Tell me what the problem is, if I am not interfering with your personal life"

"For some reasons, Kate doesn't like the parrot. She says it has an evil eye"

"Evil eyes? OK then"

"She said either me or the parrot. If I don't get rid of the parrot I can't stay with her. She said she had the right to send anyone whom she doesn't like out of her home"

"Couldn't you give the parrot away and stay with Kate?"

"No"

"May I know why?"

"No. I can't say but one day you will know. It's a very valid and important reason. Nothing personal at all"

"You make me curious to know more"

"Have I ever behaved in a way that was not rational?"

"Not at all. On the contrary, you have even been knighted by the Queen"

"There we are. Remember what I said. It is a valid, sensible and important reason"

"Very interesting"

"This parrot is important. It's precious. Not to me but to this country. I believe I have said enough"

~Chapter 9~

The Fugitive

On the next day Ed returned home to find out his house had been broken into. He thought he had had a burglary. The back door to his sitting room was broken. He immediately called the police. While waiting for the police he was happy to find the parrot was safe in place and not touched. The police arrived and investigated Ed's house, to find that nothing was stolen although everything was overturned and in a ruinously messy condition. There was money in the house but it was untouched. The police came to the conclusion that it was not a burglary, but that the intruder must have been looking for some documents. On the next day Ed telephoned Mr Davies the Energy Secretary and asked to see him urgently. In the evening Ed went to see Mr Davies

"My house was broken into yesterday but nothing was stolen. The intruder even left the cash in the house untouched. The police concluded that the intruder was looking for documents.

Accordingly I am asking for tightened security"

"That can be arranged immediately"

"I feel my life is in danger"

"As from now you will be under surveillance so no worry. I can arrange that immediately. However if you give me an hour, I shall discuss the matter with security and let you know of further action if required"

"There is one other matter which is rather serious and with which I need your co-operation. I kept all the information about the project and the plans saved on an encrypted USB stick and a CD which are stored in a bank safe box. My concern was that if I kept the PIN numbers anywhere there would be the danger of someone finding them. This was proven by what happened to my house. So I had only one choice, which will never come to be suspected by anyone or come to anyone's notice. I have a parrot which is very well trained to memorise numbers. I taught it the PIN numbers and provided a cue. If the parrot hears this cue, it will tell you the number"

"That is very clever of you, Sir Edward"

"But there are now two problems. One is this parrot needs attention and special care because it will be vulnerable to being stolen since my house was broken into"

"Was the parrot stolen or hurt?"

"Thank God, no. However this could happen at any time. Currently the parrot is in my house, but if the secret is discovered and spread around it may be stolen. In any case I don't want the parrot to be hurt because it is now valuable to the country. Like a computer it has stored the information. The other problem which is more serious is my wife who can't stand the parrot and it contributed to her depression which happened after she had an ectopic pregnancy"

"I am sorry to hear about that"

"The worst is to come. My wife and I are now separated. This is because I refused to get rid of the parrot owing to my loyalty to the country and the fact that the parrot is a vital source of information hence a valuable national asset to the United Kingdom. I love my wife and I need to go back to her especially with her current state of health. The problem is, I can't return to her with the parrot. I am living in a dilemma!

"Sir Edward. We must find a solution to this problem. Do you want me to talk to your wife?"

"No, please, don't. She doesn't know anything about the project or the relation of the parrot to the project. The parrot can't be left anywhere because it needs continuous training to memorise the PIN numbers"

"Sir Edward. Give me an hour to discuss this matter with our security. The matter seems to be serious. We shall resume our discussion subsequently"

After an hour Mr Davies had another conference with Ed

"Our security services have given instructions to place you and the parrot in premises of their choice. Usually these are away from Slough, maybe in central London. Usually the premises will be changed weekly. This is in order to avoid a fixed address being discovered, which might make you vulnerable. Someone from Scotland Yard will meet you shortly in order to discuss this matter. You will then be accompanied to your house to take what you need of your belongings.

"Mr Davies. It seems I shall be living as a fugitive"

"I am afraid so. We apologise but it's mainly for your security and to avoid any unexpected and unpleasant event. During this period our investigations will be ongoing. Also change your mobile telephone number immediately in order to avoid receiving threats or being contacted. You will also be provided with a temporary car"

Subsequently, Ed had a meeting with an officer from Scotland Yard who accompanied him to his house where he took some of his belongings and the parrot then went to stay in a flat for one week as arranged by the Energy Secretary.

Ahmad telephoned Kate and told her that Ed was very sincere and that he loved her. Ed had to keep the parrot for a very valid reason because the parrot was valuable to the United Kingdom, but Ahmad was unaware of any more information. He also told her that Ed's life was at risk and that his house had been broken into. Kate became worried about Ed. She phoned him, but because he had changed his telephone number, Kate had no reply, so she became more worried. She then drove to Ed's house and rang the bell, but there was no answer. She phoned Ahmad, who himself had no information about Ed. Kate's worry about Ed increased. Kate's condition changed from depression to anxiety, which added significant stress. She began to put the blame on herself for forcing Ed to leave her house.

On the next day, Kate had a visit from her only friend, the pharmacist Karen.
"How is your depression now?"
"Improving, but something happened recently which made me rather anxious"
"You have a very caring husband who will look after you, besides your mum, who is here now"
"Ed has left home"

"Impossible. He is very sensible"

"I gave him the green light to go. In fact the truth is that I asked him to leave"

"Why?"

"He has a parrot which has an evil looking eye and which I couldn't stand. I asked Ed to get rid of the parrot but he refused. He left because I said either me or the parrot and he preferred to keep the parrot"

"That's very strange, to favour a bird over his wife. I wonder why "

"I don't know exactly. The last thing I heard from a friend of his is that the parrot was very important and that it was a valuable national asset to the United Kingdom. Imagine, Karen, a parrot being a valuable national asset to the country. Would you believe it?"

"How would a parrot become a valuable national asset to the country? It must be very valuable. But why to the country?"

"Ed is a sensible person. He doesn't talk nosense. What he says is the truth"

"Yep. That makes it more complicated. There must be something behind that parrot. God knows what it is"

"A rather strange thing happened two days ago. That is why I am worried about Ed. His house was broken into during the day but nothing was stolen. The police said that the intruder must have been looking for some documents"

"Documents?! What sort of documents?"

"God knows. My husband is involved in various big projects from all over the world. I was wondering if there was an attempt to steal some documents related to these overseas countries. The important matter now is I lost contact completely with Ed. He is not at home nor can I contact him by telephone. I don't know what happened to him. I am so worried"

Her friend Karen went back home and explained the events to her husband. Karen's husband expressed interest in this case, particularly the part about the parrot and the expression of "a valuable national asset to the United Kingdom" used to describe the parrot.

Kate phoned Ahmad to obtain information about Ed, but Ahmad told her that he had not seen him on that day in the company and his telephone number was unobtainable. Kate contacted the police, who reported no accident or incident had happened in which Ed was involved.

Two days later, Kate phoned Ahmad during the day. Ahmad told her that Ed was seen at work that day. She decided to go and see him in his office. His PA told Kate that he could see her at 6.oopm in his office. Upon arrival at 6.oo pm Kate was informed that Ed had to leave for an urgent meeting but Ed's PA was unable to tell Kate where. It took Ed's PA by surprise when she saw Kate requesting to meet her husband in his office making an appointment through his PA, but she wasn't in a position to comment. Kate had no choice but to phone Ahmad again:

"Ahmad. I need your help. Please tell Ed I want to see him urgently. Tell him I am rather worried about him. He seems not to be living in his home. No contact telephone number"

"Yes, you are right. I think he has changed his telephone number because I can't contact him either. I will tell him when I see him at work, hopefully tomorrow."

Ahmad did not have the chance to see Ed on the following day because Ed was out of the company most of the day. Kate kept phoning Ahmad asking for information about Ed but without any luck. Kate's concentration at work was severely jeopardised. She therefore cancelled her operation list during that week in order to avoid any problems to her patients. Three days later Kate managed to see Ed in his office after waiting for him in his PA's office for a few hours. It was after 7.00 pm when Kate entered Ed's office and stared at him, standing with tears flowing from her eyes

"Shut the door behind you, please," said Ed, rising from his seat behind his desk and staring at his wife

"No hugs! No kisses!" said Kate

"Hello, Kate. What a surprise! It's nice to see you"

"Have you no heart? Are you emotionless?"

"You broke my heart, but in a different way. You broke it when I loved you dearly and now you have broken it in to pieces when you kicked me out of your house"

"I do apologise. It was a mistake I committed. I repent"

"I am glad you have learnt your lesson," said Ed, who knew he loved Kate dearly but he wanted to stand firm, as he did before against his desire, in order to teach Kate a lesson not to be stubborn in difficult situations. But Ed also was aware that Kate had some right to ask him to leave with the parrot at a time when she was ill and was under the impression that the parrot had contributed to her illness.

"Come on, Ed. Kiss me. Hug me. Hold me. Squeeze me. I need you. I need you desperately"

Ed went round his desk and approached Kate, who was standing waiting for Ed to come near to her. Ed stopped a metre from her, looking at her. Kate closed her eyes and protruded her lips, waiting for a hug and a kiss from Ed, who stood firm in his place. Kate then opened her eyes and looked at Ed

"I said sorry. Isn't that enough?" said Kate

Ed shook his head

"What do you want then?"

Ed kept staring at her in silence, waiting for her to come closer to him

"Ed. I am a lady. I suffered a lot. I wish you would realise the stress and anxiety which I have suffered in the past few days because of you. I need you. I need your warmth"

Kate's words affected Ed deeply. He realised that she had had enough of suffering. Ed stepped closer to her. Kate closed her eyes and waited for further action from Ed. His emotion peaked and his heart rate began to increase. He put his arms round her shoulders and pulled her towards him, then placed his left palm at the back of her head and placed his left cheek over her left cheek and started rubbing her head soothingly. At that point Kate felt restful and happy. She was in the arms of her beloved husband, who she had eventually discovered was in a sound state and normal, safe in one piece and unharmed. She then pushed his head gently and brought her lips nearer to his, then gave him a long kiss. This brought both Ed and Kate calm and all the bad feeling started to fade away.

"I won't leave tonight until you accompany me to my place"

"I can't do it"

"Why not?! I did apologise, didn't I? My apologies again and again"

"Let's sit down and talk".

Kate and Ed sat down.

"Listen, Kate. This is not easy as you may think"

"Why not?! Am I not your wife?"

"Yes, you are. I am not denying that"

"What is the problem then?"

"It is beyond my control"

"I can't understand"

"It is rather complicated for security reasons"

"What security? You are scaring me"

"Didn't you hear that my house was broken into?"

"Yes, I know, that's why I want you to come with me. My house is yours. Come on, let's go"

"My dear, Kate. It's not as simple as you may think. I can't tell you more than what I have already said"

"So you are hiding something. OK where are you living now?"

"I can't say"

"You are living with a woman. Aren't you?"

"Is that what your explanation is? If it is, you are absolutely crazy. You know very well that the last thing in my life I think of is women"

"Why don't you tell me where you live now?"

"Because I can't. Because I was told not to say anything"

"There must be a reason"

"Yes, there is a reason, but I can't talk for security reasons"

"I am becoming nervous now. I am worried about you"

"Don't get nervous and don't be worried"

"Come with me, then"

"We are back to square one. I wish I could"

Kate's mobile phone rang. She picked it up to find the caller was her mother. Kate spoke in Portuguese

"Hello. Yes, it's me" Kate opened her eyes widely in surprise "Come on, Mum, talk. What is the matter with you?... Oh my God!..Are you OK?....Knife?...What knife?...No...what...parrot..You   say parrot?!..OK. I will be with you soon"

Kate closed the mobile phone and immediately turned her face to Ed

"My house was broken into from the back garden. Two men entered and my mum was held at knife point by one of them while the other man went to the first floor. After a while he came down and they were talking to Mum, but all she understood was they were saying to her 'parrot' few times then they left the premises. Ed, I must go. My mum is in a terrible state"

"Just be patient." Ed stopped her from leaving "I know what is going on"

Ed picked up his mobile phone and called the Energy Secretary

"Mr Davies. It's Ed Carpenter. My wife's house has just been broken into by two men...Yes, she is fine, she is here with me in my office, thank God, but her mother is at home. My mother-in-law phoned my wife to say she had been held at knife point by two men. The interesting thing is they were talking to her in English but all what she could understand was they kept saying to her 'parrot' 'parrot'.....This is becoming serious. I want to go with my wife to her house...Do you agree that I should take my wife and her mother to stay with me?...Yes, I will. I shall go outside the building now"

Ed finished his call then turned his head to Kate

"You will come with me now and we shall go in your car to your house. The police will be there. You and your mother will come and live with me until further notice"

Kate took Ed in her car and drove to her house, where two police car were waiting. They entered the house and saw Kate's mother sitting on a chair shaking. Kate and Ed rushed to Kate's mother. Kate hugged her mother and spoke to her in Portuguese. The police entered and searched the house. Kate went to the first floor, where she shouted

"Oh! My God. They turned everything upside down"

Kate later came down the stairs to say, "Very strange. All my jewellery and money is in place. I don't know what they were looking for"

"I do know," said Ed "Good, Kate, that you were not at home"

A policewoman sat down with Ed and Kate to interrogate Kate, who was shaking. Ed was holding Kate with his arms around her shoulders.

"We learned they were saying 'Parrot' to your mother. Can your mother confirm this?"

Kate translated what the policewoman was saying to Portuguese. Kate's mother then spoke

"Yes both men were talking in English, but all she understood was 'Parrot'" said Kate

"How did she not remember any word apart from 'parrot'?" said the policewoman

"Because we had a parrot at home for a few months and my mum knew this word because my husband and I mentioned the name frequently in front of her," said Kate

"What is particular about the parrot? It seems the men were looking for it," said the policewoman

"That is what I suspect," said Ed

"I still don't understand. Can you provide any explanation as to why the intruders were looking for a parrot?" said the police woman

"This is a security matter, Officer. I can't say. I shall give you the telephone number of an officer in Scotland Yard, who will explain to you if you so wish," said Ed

"Yes, please. Give me the telephone number," said the Police woman.

Ed gave her the telephone number then the police woman went into a corner to phone the officer in Scotland Yard

"Ed. There is something going on which I am unaware of and it's to do with the parrot," said Kate

"That is why the parrot was so important"

"But you did not explain"

"I couldn't at the time"

"Tell me now"

"I still can't. Just be patient, please. You will know everything one day"

"It's good that the parrot was not in my house"

"It's good, but I didn't know anyone knew about the parrot's importance except me. I wonder how those two men knew and came looking for it! It's very strange"

The policewoman came to Ed and Kate after talking to the Scotland Yard officer.

"OK. I have been given all the information. Lady Carpenter and your mother will leave the house and go to stay with you, Sir Edward until further notice," said the Policewoman

"Officer. I am surprised those men knew about the parrot. I haven't spoken to anyone about it," said Ed

The policewoman then started interrogating Kate

"Lady Carpenter. What is your job?"

"I am a consultant ophthalmologist"

"Where do you work?"

"Moorfield Hospital"

"Have you seen anyone or spoken to any person recently?"

"Yes, to my husband"

"Apart from your husband, did you speak to anyone else?"

Kate looked at Ed then at the Policewoman

"Yes, I did"

"To whom?"

"To Ahmad, my husband's friend"

"What did you tell him?"

"I just asked him about my husband. I was worried about my husband. I wanted to know where he was. Nothing special"

Ed jumped in to say,

"The parrot was a gift from Ahmad. He doesn't have any further information"

"Did you speak to another person and mention about the parrot?" asked the policewoman

"Yes, to a friend of mine called Karen Rogers. She is a pharmacist whom I have known for twelve years"

"When did you last see her?"

"May be a week ago"

"Where did you see her?"

"She came to visit me at home"

"What did you talk about in particular?"

"I told her about my husband leaving home"

"Do you remember if you mentioned the parrot to her or anything about the parrot?"

"Yes." Kate turned her head to Ed. "Forgive me, Ed." Then turned her head to the policewoman "I told her it was because of the parrot that my husband left home. I told her the parrot was very important to him and that this was something which I didn't understand. I said there must have been something secret about the parrot, which I found peculiar. Once I saw my husband talking quietly to the parrot as if he was hiding something from me"

"Did you tell that to your friend?"

"Yes, I did"

"Did you have to say all that to her?" said Ed

"I am sorry, Ed, it was a mistake. But I trusted my friend," said Kate

"We need to investigate this, but do you think your friend had any link to what happened?"

"I doubt it. I have known her for a long time"

"Is she married?"

"Yes"

"Do you know her husband?"

"I have only seen him two or three times"

"Do you know her address?"

"Yes"

"We shall need the address"

Kate gave the address to the policewoman. The police asked Kate and her mother to take their clothes and enough other belongings for a few days and leave the house and be escorted by them to Ed's temporary apartment. Kate was pleased that her husband had returned to her although she was eager to learn the reason for Ed to live at a secret address.

Kate's mother was in such a devastated state of shock after the event and kept asking to leave London and go back to Lisbon. Ed, Kate and her mother left the premises and were escorted by the police to Ed's temporary premises. Kate very happily spent the night alongside Ed, whom she had missed for a few weeks. The following morning, Ed received a call from Scotland Yard to be ready to move to new premises. Kate's mother insisted she wanted to return to Lisbon. Kate booked her a flight back on the same day and took her to the airport. Like fugitives, Ed and Kate moved on that evening to another temporary apartment selected by the police in the centre of London.

~Chapter 10~

The Parrot Kate and Ed

I nvestigation of the events of the break-in at Kate's house started immediately. The police thoroughly investigated Kate's friend, Karen Rogers, who apparently was the only person Kate was in contact with. The information that Kate passed to Karen made the police suspicious of Karen and her family. It was found that Karen had two little children of six and eight and that her 45-year-old husband was a sales agent for a cloth company. He made frequent journeys to European countries as part of his profession but also made a few trips to countries in South America. This news gave the police no clue and did not provide any evidence that Mr Rogers had any link to the events surrounding the attack on Kate's house. However the police continued their interest in conducting further investigations and kept Ed and Kate informed of the progress.

Because Ed learned that Kate had passed some information to her friend Karen, he kept all the information about the project and the parrot secret within himself, away from Kate. On the third night after her return to Ed, she was lying down in bed with her head and hair over Ed's arm. Kate's left cheek was touching Ed's chest. She felt relaxed, breathing in his odour.

"You did not inform me of what's going on," said Kate, putting her right palm over Ed's left cheek and softly increasing his emotion and desire.

"Please, Kate. It's not time yet. One day you will know everything, but all I ask is please don't talk to anyone about anything, especially the parrot".

"This makes me rather curious to know more"

"I wish you realised the difficulty and the suffering I have been going through. We have to be patient in all the circumstances. I am certain when everything is over you will be very pleased"

"Do you think that there will be a good outcome?"

"I hope so, but there is no guarantee"

"We are living like fugitives"

"At least we are both together under the same roof"

"And on the same bed"

"And you are in my arms"

Ed then gave Kate a kiss, which gave her an agreeable feeling of relaxation. She could not wait to have Ed pressed to her bare body to satisfy and fulfil her sexual desire. She felt very joyful. Within herself, Kate was more in favour of becoming pregnant again, especially after her ectopic pregnancy rather than just fulfilling her sexual desire.

"Do you know what, Ed? I am dreaming of becoming pregnant again"

"Be patient. It will happen one day. It's just a matter of chance"

"I would love to have another Ed in my tummy"

"Do you mean a dyslexic Ed?"

"I mean Sir Edward"

"I like that. I like your optimistic outlook"

"This is what I learned from you"

"Yes. Despite being dyslexic I have never been pessimistic in my life, even when I didn't get what I was hoping for and even if things went against my wishes. This was one of the reasons for my success in life"

On the following evening, Ed received a call from the Energy Secretary inviting him and Kate on Saturday evening to a secret dinner party restricted to all those involved in the project and the party guest of honour was the Prime Minister. Ed thought it was time for him to inform Kate about his role in the project so that she learned to be discreet and would not be surprised during the dinner party. He thought that the best time to talk would be when both were relaxed in bed on Friday night.

"Darling, Kate. You have asked me numerous times about the reasons for those events which have taken place. Will you be able to keep a secret?"

"I am surprised at what you are saying. Am I not your beloved wife who is loyal to you?"

"Promise me you won't tell anyone intentionally or non-intentionally. Nothing at all. Promise me also to honour your promise"

Kate removed her head from his arms and looked at him in surprise

"If you promise me, not only shall I tell you things, but I will also give you a treat"

"What is the treat?"

"It will come later. Something you are eager to have"

"You are naughty," said Kate with a smile

"You and I are invited tomorrow evening to a party"

"That's good. We have never been invited together except once by Ahmad and once by the chairman"

"That was history. This is important. Do you know who the host is?"

"Who is the host?"

"It's the Energy Secretary and the Prime Minister will be the guest of honour"

"That's good but what do you have to do with the Energy Secretary? Is it a project that you have done or plans you have made for the Energy Secretary? I am just joking"

"No you are not joking. It's the truth"

"Oh, really. Is this part of your secret?"

"Yes indeed. The whole project was secret. It was top secret because it was in the interest of the United Kingdom as a whole"

"You are making me excited. Tell me more"

"I won't give you more information because tomorrow you will hear more about it. Tomorrow I shall give a 15-minute presentation. There will be three more presentations including an introduction by the Energy Secretary"

"I am really excited for you, Ed. Having a husband of that calibre is an advantage and a credit for me"

"Do you know what the best credit is?"

"What is it?"

"Is to keep this shut," said Ed, placing his fingers on Kate's mouth "You will be very excited tomorrow after knowing what is really going on"

"I can't wait until tomorrow. But you should have told me before so that I could choose a suitable dress"

"We will go tomorrow morning to buy you one"

"Is anyone else aware of this?"

"Like who?"

"Like your friend Ahmad"

"No one knows anything. My involvement was entirely personal and private. If it wasn't for this project I wouldn't have come to know you!"

"How is that?"

"Do you remember when I first came to see you for a consultation?"

"How can I forget that happy day?"

"I was heavily involved in that project. It caused me stress and lack of sleep. I had to take four weeks' holiday from work in order to work solely on that project"

"And what does the parrot have to do with it?"

"That is the big secret which I shall explain as soon as everything is settled and the police investigation is complete. The parrot is the key to everything"

"Don't tell me that that defenceless bird which is in a cage has a strong relation to a secret project which is of a national interest to the United Kingdom!!"

"I am afraid that it is the case"

Kate's surprise reached its peak and her eagerness to learn about that secret was enormous. However that discussion with Ed made her feel more kind towards the parrot and interested in preserving its health and welfare.

It took Ed by surprise when he woke up in the morning to find Kate in her nightdress near the parrot's cage talking and whispering to it. He was happy to see that scene. It had never happened before.

"I see you are talking to the parrot," said Ed

"It's so lovely. Look at it."

"I am glad you like it"

"Why wouldn't I like it? At least it keeps saying, ' I love you, Kate'"

"Let's have breakfast and go and buy you a dress for tonight's event"

After breakfast Ed and Kate went out to buy a dress. When they came back home Ed was updating his powerpoint slide presentation on his plans for the project.

Kate and Ed arrived at the party venue. They received a warm welcome from the Energy Secretary and his wife. In the reception they met all the people involved in the project including the scientists and the physicists. When the Prime Minister arrived with his wife he was introduced to all those in attendance by the Energy Secretary and came to meet Ed

"Please meet Sir Edward Carpenter and Lady Carpenter, who is also known as Miss Kate Fernandes a consultant ophthalmologist"

"It's nice to see you. I heard a lot about you and your achievement Sir Edward. We are very proud to meet one of the very loyal people to the United Kingdom"

"It's nice to meet you too"

"I am very sorry to hear about what happened to you and I hope we shall finish the investigation in a reasonable time"

After the reception the delegates were taken to a small lecture room. The Energy Secretary gave a small introductory remark. This was followed by a short speech from the Prime Minister

"It is my pleasure to welcome you this evening. You have made a rather important achievement to the United Kingdom and the British population. The project which will be constructed will have a significant impact on the price of electricity.."

To this end Kate turned her head to Ed with a smile and held his hand then she continued to listen to the speech of the Prime Minister

"..and eventually every one now, our children and all the future generations will benefit as you may imagine. Not only that but the unique innovation which our scientists have invented will make the United Kingdom in a strong financial position when we start selling electricity to the rest of the European countries"

Kate looked at Ed with a surprising sign on her face switching off from the Prime

Minister's speech. Ed looked at her with a smile then she continued listening

"..I would like to thank all those involved in the project, those who innovated the idea and the scientific invention, Sir Edward Carpenter who made the plans of the building and Mr Robert Waterman who did the structural engineering work. I must say that the plan was an amazing idea. We still have to admit that we should keep the whole project secret. There are countries and organisation which would love to have such an invention on their lands. Accordingly, we have to be careful not to expose any of the ideas, plans etcetera to anyone. The other concern is any act of terrorism which might take place during construction. The plans to steal the idea have already begun and some of you have already suffered. Our security forces, however, are taking serious steps to combat such activities and I am certain we shall be able to diffuse any such attempt. May I wish you all a very lovely evening"

The Prime Minister was applauded then he sat down. His speech was followed by a presentation from one of the scientists to show the principle of the invention and its significance. When he finished, Ed turned his head to Kate and said

"It's now my turn to speak"

The Energy Secretary stood up and went on the stage to say

"We have just received a note from our security to advise that the next speech to be delivered by Sir Edward Carpenter is to be cancelled for security reasons. Our apologies but I hope you understand the seriousness of the issue. Now please Ladies and gentleman may we all go for dinner"

Ed was not surprised for the announcement of the Energy Secretary but Kate was disappointed when she heard that

"No!.. I am disappointed. I wanted to see you on the stage and I was eager to see your plans" Said Kate.

All the delegate went for dinner. The Energy Secretary took Ed to one side and asked him in private

"I just want to know if you had told your wife about the plans which you drew for the project and the secret which you are still holding"

"Not at all. I think we agreed in the beginning that this matter was a top secret"

"Many thanks Sir Edward. I just wanted to confirm only. It is also for your security"

"I understand"

"I am sorry that you may have to be moved to another place until the investigation is complete and we reach a conclusion. It's for your safety"

After dinner Kate and Ed went home which they have to leave and move to another apartment on the following day. They continued moving to a different apartment every one or two weeks for two months.

Kate woke up one day to feel sick which continued for a few days. She had two missed periods and found she had a positive pregnancy test.

"Ed. I am pregnant again. I can't believe it. I am carrying your child. I hope it is not an ectopic pregnancy this time"

One week later, Ed received a telephone call from the Energy Secretary asking him to have a meeting urgently. Ed went to see Mr Davies who said

"Sir Edward. I have very good news not just to you but to all of us. The investigations have been completed. They found that there was a big plot. However, we don't know if it was a terrorist organisation or trying to steal the idea but most likely the gang was commissioned by another country to steal the idea. That is why they were looking for the parrot"

"Even if they capture the parrot. They still can't get any information"

"Can you explain please?"

"I will just tell you that if they want to get any information either me or the parrot is not enough. It has to be both of us together, the parrot and me"

"Can you explain please?"

"We shall explain later"

"The security informed me that you can now go back to you or your wife's house. There is no more danger. You are free!"

"What about the parrot?"

"We have decided to take the responsibility of storing the data and the plan. The security will look after that and the information will be stored in a safe place. The Prime Minister will see you specifically to thank you and award you for all your efforts"

"That is highly appreciated"

"The appreciation is for your loyalty to the United kingdom. You have already been knighted and I think the Prime Minister is considering recommending you for the House of Lords"

"I have to hand in all the original project plans and work"

"I shall let you know when we are going to visit the Prime Minister at number 10"

"Thanks a lot"

"Thanks for all your efforts. Construction work will start soon"

Kate and Ed moved to Kate's house without any fear or concern. They took the parrot with them. Kate's pregnancy was normal and she had a scan which showed it was a normal uterine pregnancy.

Kate eventually came to recognise the struggle that her dyslexic husband, Ed had to do in order to fulfil his desire in life and being knighted. She learnt that defending his principles and his loyalty to his country were great achievement. The experience she had from Ed of patience and perseverance and to let her personal emotional desires supervened by her principles and being loyal to her principles were the best achievement she acquired in her life.

Ed was smiling when he said "I am pleased that the parrot my wife and I are back under the same roof. It was the parrot which contributed to my learning to be loyal to my country and my principles. There are lots that you can learn from anyone even an innocent animal like a parrot.

Kate was overwhelmed by carrying Ed's child in her tummy. She was hoping that the child would follow the track of Ed to struggle in life and being loyal to one's country and principles.

~Author Bio~

Abdul-Majeed Salmasi is an NHS London-based consultant cardiologist and researcher in cardiovascular medicine. He is a Clinical Senior Lecturer at the National Heart and Lung Institute of the Imperial College London. He obtained his Ph.D. in Medicine from St Mary's Hospital Medical School, London University. He is a fellow of different professional medical colleges and societies. His other qualifications as a Master Practitioner in Neurolinguistic programming and clinical hypnotherapist made his hobby of writing short stories to evolve to writing novels. He uses his experience in understanding the psychology and pathology in his novels. Most of all, his novels contain some medical conditions which are important in people's lives.